Stormy Fall

Stormy Fall

Betty Barclift

Kregel Publications

Stormy Fall: A Novel

© 2004 by Betty Barclift

Published by Kregel Publications, a division of Kregel, Inc., P.O. Box 2607, Grand Rapids, MI 49501.

All rights reserved. No part of this book may be reproduced, stored in a retrieval system, or transmitted in any form or by any means—electronic, mechanical, photocopy, recording, or otherwise—without written permission of the publisher, except for brief quotations in printed reviews.

This book is a work of fiction. Names, characters, places, and incidents are either the product of the author's imagination or are used fictitiously. Any resemblance to actual events or locales or persons, living or dead, is entirely coincidental.

Library of Congress Cataloging-in-Publication Data
Barclift, Betty.
   Stormy fall: a novel /by Betty Barclift.
      p.   cm.
      [1. Toleration—Fiction. 2. Homeless persons—Fiction. 3. Schools—Fiction. 4. Christian life—Fiction. 5. Family life—Washington (State)—Fiction. 6. Washington (State)—Fiction.] I. Title.
PZ7.B245St 2004
[Fic]—dc22   2004020964

ISBN 0-8254-2028-8

Printed in the United States of America
04 05 06 07 08 / 5 4 3 2 1

Stormy Fall

Chapter One

*K*atie Barnes heard the soft crunch of yellow and brown maple leaves under her feet as she quickly made her way across the church lawn. The junior high youth-group meeting would start in five minutes, and she didn't want to walk in late. She shivered and crammed her fists into the pockets of her thin blue windbreaker. Burrrr! This October fog was cold. Spooky, too.

"Katie? Katie Barnes, is that you?" croaked a ghostly voice through the fog.

Katie's heart beat faster. She whirled around and squinted to see who was following her, but all she saw through the fog and darkness were the blurry taillights of a car leaving the parking lot. Finally, she spied a faint figure jogging toward her across the lawn. The closer he got, the brighter his red-orange hair became.

"Tim!" she said in a shaky voice. "You practically scared me to death, coming up behind me like that!"

Tim Reilly, a tall and gangly fourteen-year-old, bounded up beside her. "Sorry, Katie. I didn't mean to scare you. Guess it's the fog."

Katie made a face. "So far, I'm not liking this western Washington weather very much. First, the rain last summer almost washed away our tent, and now we have this...."

"Yeah, my Uncle Sean says this is the nastiest fall he's ever seen around Mapleton." Tim zipped up his windbreaker. "I think the cool weather and fog is caused by westerly winds blowing across unusually cold ocean currents just offshore in the Pacific, and then—"

"Please, Tim," begged Katie. "No meteorology lesson tonight, okay? My teeth are already chattering."

Tim covered up his obvious disappointment with a little grin. "Okay, no weather talk. Guess I get a little carried away. Weather's just so interesting that I can't shut up sometimes...." He stopped talking and stared toward the church. "Hey!" he whispered. "Look over there, Katie. There's a couple of people kneeling in the flower bed. Are they praying?"

Katie looked hard toward the brightly lit front entrance. "They're not praying, Tim. Looks to me like they're digging holes." She took a few steps closer. "I think it's the Tootle sisters!" She grabbed Tim's arm. "Come on. Let's go see what our new church janitors are up to on a night like this."

Edith and Stella Tootle both looked around as Tim and Katie joined them. Their old faces were crisscrossed with wrinkles and smudged with freshly dug soil. Their tangled gray hair stood out on their heads like steel wool halos.

"Well, look who's here!" shouted Edith, waving a garden trowel. Edith was a little hard of hearing, so her voice was often loud. Her sister, Stella, only grinned, showing dark gaps where teeth were missing.

"You two ladies probably shouldn't be working outside in the dark," said Tim. "Especially in this fog."

Curious, Katie hunkered down beside them and looked at the empty flower bed. "What have you been planting in all these holes, Edith?"

Edith popped a big brown bulb into a hole and covered it with soil. "Why, we're planting spring sunshine, Katie. Come next March, this bed'll be one big mass of yellow daffodils. And won't that be pretty?"

"It sure will," agreed Katie. "But Tim's right. You and Stella probably should be heading back to your motel before the fog gets worse. Should I find someone to drive you?"

The two old women looked at each other and shook their heads. "Oh, no, we've got everything taken care of," Edith said. She snatched up her trowel and an empty paper sack. "We were just getting ready to leave. Come on, Stella." They both started walking out into the darkness.

"Don't forget, Mom's expecting both of you at our house for Thanksgiving dinner," Katie called after them.

"Oh, we'll be there—that's a promise," said Edith with a chuckle. Stella only smiled and waved her hand as they disappeared into the night.

"Stella doesn't say much, does she?" said Tim.

"Edith says she's just shy." Katie almost skipped as she tried to keep pace with Tim's long legs. "Edith and Stella are really neat old ladies," she continued. "I think it's been good for the whole church to have them as our janitors. When we get the Good Samaritan Homeless Shelter going, the church members won't be afraid of the homeless folks anymore. They'll know they're just like them."

Stormy Fall

"*If* we get a homeless shelter going here, Katie, not *when*." Tim started up the steps of the side entrance to their youth-group classroom with Katie at his heels.

"What do you mean, 'if'?" argued Katie. "The church board voted to turn the Foster house into a homeless shelter last week. It's a done deal."

"Not until the trustees okay it," said Tim. "Church bylaws say nothing can be done without their consent. They're having their meeting here tonight to decide."

"Oh, no," groaned Katie. "With Phoebe Phillips as chairperson of the trustees, we know how their vote'll go, don't we?"

Tim's answer was drowned out by the eardrum-bursting sounds of screeching brakes, clashing metal, and shattering glass on the road below.

Katie clamped her hands over her ears. "What was that?"

"It sounded like a car crash!" Tim dashed through the foggy darkness toward the road with Katie trailing him. The side door of the church burst open, and the rest of the junior high kids rushed outside and followed them down to the roadway.

Within minutes, a red and white car pulled to a stop, sirens blaring. Two patrol cars joined them, their flashing red and blue lights slicing through the fog. Traffic was at a standstill.

"What happened?" shouted Shad Emery.

"Yeah, what's going on?" asked his cousin, Alisha Asher.

Ed Kipper, one of the youth-group leaders, hurried out of the darkness, the beam of his flashlight bouncing wildly. "Stand back, everybody! Let's let the patrolmen and medics do their jobs, okay?" The group of kids lining the roadway pulled back an inch or two.

Stormy Fall

Katie stood on tiptoe in an effort to see the fearsome sight out on the road. Finally, she glimpsed a large pickup and a scrunched and battered car. Rescue workers were working furiously to free someone from inside the green car. Katie gasped and turned to Shad Emery, who was standing behind her.

"Shad, do you know if Phoebe Phillips has shown up for that trustees' meeting yet?"

"I don't know, Katie," said Shad. "Why?"

A shiver went up Katie's backbone. "Because that wrecked car looks like her green Cadillac."

Tall Shad craned his neck and looked over everybody's heads. "Oh, no. I think you're right!" The flashing lights showed the shock on his dark face. "Looks like that big pickup squashed her car like a tin can!"

None of the gathered crowd spoke as the medics finally freed the person inside the wreck. Like mute puppets, each head turned as the uniformed medics gently eased the person onto a stretcher and began carrying the stretcher toward the waiting ambulance.

"It *is* Phoebe!" said Katie. "I hope she's all right. She's so still!"

But as the ambulance doors swung open, the figure on the stretcher moved and even struggled to sit up. "That . . . that truck driver . . ." Her head dropped back onto the stretcher. She stopped to catch her breath. "He—he deliberately ran into my car!" She moaned.

"Now, now," soothed the medic.

But Phoebe didn't want to be soothed. "Call my attorney this minute!" she gasped. "And call my cousin Ellison Simms! And the newspaper!"

Stormy Fall

As she grew more and more upset, Pastor Miller hurried to her side. He clasped her thin, shaking hand between his two big ones. "You're going to be just fine, Phoebe. We're all praying for you."

"Oh, Pastor Miller, please talk to the other trustees," Phoebe begged weakly. "Tell them they cannot hold their meeting tonight without me. They cannot vote for . . ." Her voice faded as medics eased her into the ambulance and closed the doors. The ambulance slowly rolled away.

By now the driver of the big pickup was out and sitting by the side of the road, assuring medics he was all right. He leaned his head back against a tree trunk. "I couldn't help it," he said sadly to the patrolmen. "That car cut right across in front of me without signaling. It just darted out of the fog. I'm so sorry. I hope the lady's okay." Pastor Miller and the medics patted his burly shoulders and spoke quietly to him.

Within minutes the state patrol began routing traffic around the accident scene. Cars started up, and bystanders began walking away.

"We'd better be getting back to our youth room, guys!" said Sue Wong, president of the youth group. "We'll only be in the way around here."

Katie caught up with her good friend Alisha. "I feel so awful, Alisha! Just a second before Phoebe's accident, I was hoping she couldn't make it to that trustees' meeting tonight. Now she's on her way to the hospital." Katie shivered. "And after she was nice enough to let my family stay in her apartment when we were homeless last summer, too."

Alisha nodded her head, her springy black curls bounc-

Stormy Fall

ing up and down. "A lot of us are feeling a little guilty right now. No one would have wanted Phoebe to get hurt, but it sure has been hard to like her lately. She's been doing everything she can to stop plans for a homeless shelter.

"Anyway, we know Phoebe can still move and talk, and that means a lot. I'll bet she'll be fine."

Back in the lighted and heated youth room, everybody wanted to talk.

Claudia Curtiss, a ninth-grader whose family were longtime friends of Phoebe's, sat down at the long table. Ignoring the other kids, she took a small cell phone from her purse, brushed back her frizzed reddish-blond hair, punched in some numbers, and clamped the phone against her ear. While the others sat and glared at her, she began describing the car accident to an unseen friend.

"Uh-huh, that's right . . . and poor Phoebe was carried away on a stretcher," she babbled. "I hope she sues that truck driver. He totaled her beautiful Cadillac."

"Sue the truck driver?" scoffed Shad. "It's not like the poor guy could help it. She cut him off!"

"And everyone knows Phoebe Phillips always drives like she owns the road," Mark Gomez said. He stuffed the last half of a chocolate-covered nut bar into his mouth and began chewing.

Finally, Tim Reilly joined them and sat down beside Shad. "I just saw a couple of the church trustees drive away," he said. "It looks like they did cancel their meeting tonight."

"At least we know the trustees won't be voting down the homeless-shelter project tonight," said Alisha. "And who knows? Maybe they'll eventually approve it."

Stormy Fall

"No way," said a voice at the far end of the table. Michael Vincent had been ignoring the talk while he pecked at his small, expensive laptop computer. Now he looked up, and the overhead light reflected off his thick-lensed glasses.

"Get real, guys. Whether the trustees vote tonight or next week, they're going to vote down the Good Samaritan Homeless Shelter. They're not going to cross Phoebe Phillips. Besides, do any of us really want dangerous homeless people living right next door to our church building?"

Katie was reminded once again of her own family's homeless summer. She jumped to her feet. "Dangerous! What's so dangerous about homeless people? A few of them, sure, but most homeless people are just like you and me. Why, if Pastor Miller hadn't found the Tootle sisters when they were sleeping in a back alley downtown, they'd be homeless today. And our church would be without two new church members and a couple of terrific custodians."

"You're right, Katie." Claudia smirked as she turned off her cell phone. "But do we want ten or twelve more people that look like them in our church services? What will visitors think? When Mrs. Foster deeded her house to the church, she only asked that it be used to help in the Lord's work. She didn't ask that we use it as a shelter for people like Edith and Stella Tootle. There are lots of ways to help in the Lord's work!"

"Oh, sure," jeered Mark. "You mean selling it and buying stained-glass windows? You think that's a better way to do the Lord's work?"

"Please, guys, let's not argue at a time like this," begged Sue. Suddenly the door opened again and youth-group leaders

14

Stormy Fall

Joan and Ed Kipper joined them. Joan held up her hand to quiet the loud voices. "I know you kids are upset and concerned," she said. "Instead of having a regular meeting tonight, Ted and I thought maybe you'd rather have a circle of prayer for Mrs. Phillips and the other driver, and then go home early."

Mark waved his hand high. "We can't do that," he protested, concern showing in his round face. "We haven't had our refreshments yet! And my mom sent a spice cake with maple-nut frosting."

"Honestly, Mark," protested Claudia. "Just because your parents own that little hole-in-the-wall restaurant downtown doesn't mean food has to be all you think about!"

Ed Kipper chuckled. "I guess it would take a mighty bad accident to cause Mark to lose his appetite. Okay, guys, let's eat before our circle of prayer."

As usual, Katie and Tim hitched a ride home after their meeting with jolly Mr. Emery and the rest of the Lower Mapleton kids. Katie squeezed into the back row of the big van between Janie Dawson, another neighborhood friend, and Alisha. No one talked much as they rode down the hill. Even Mrs. Gomez's luscious maple-nut frosting couldn't take away the memory of the accident that night, or their worry about the future of Good Samaritan House.

Janie was the first one to be dropped off at home. Her family lived in an apartment above the Dawsons' garage on the lower edge of Mapleton. Katie, on the other hand, was one of the last to be dropped off. Mr. Emery pulled into the Barnes's driveway and delivered her at her front door. "We can't have a young lady walking alone in this fog," he said when Katie thanked him.

Katie waved and watched the Emery van drive away, then turned to look at the rundown old house that had been her home for the last two months. In the misty darkness, it looked even more like a haunted house. Dad had repaired the sagging front porch, but no one had found time to paint it yet. The only light burning was a single overhead bulb in the living room. Katie remembered how ashamed she'd felt when they had moved into this old house.

So maybe our house doesn't look much like those big fancy places up on the hill, Katie thought. *But it's better than living in a tent or our minivan, and it's a whole lot better than being a missionary project for Phoebe.* She climbed the porch steps, took out her key, and unlocked the front door.

Dad was sitting in his shabby overstuffed chair, his head nodding, his eyes closed. Poor Dad. Katie knew that after dropping her off at the church, he'd driven Mom to her evening job at the Eat-A-Bite Café. Mom didn't like driving in the fog, so he would pick her up again at two in the morning, then leave for his construction job five hours later, at seven A.M.

Across the living room, their ancient television blared away. Katie tiptoed over to it and turned it off.

Her dad jerked awake. "Katie! I was watching that." Katie grinned and kissed him on his forehead. "Sorry, Dad. I thought you were asleep."

Dad chuckled. "Yeah, well . . ." He stood up stiffly and worked his shoulders to relax them. "So, how was your youth meeting, hon?"

"We didn't have much of a meeting because there was a bad accident right in front of the church." Katie told him about Phoebe's crash with the pickup. "They took Phoebe to the hospital in an ambulance. I don't know how badly she was hurt, but she could still talk."

Her dad shook his head. "Poor lady. We'll have to pray that both Phoebe and the other driver are okay. I'll check tomorrow and see if there's any way we can help her." His mouth gaped open in a big yawn. "Looks like we'd both better be heading to bed now, Katie. Goodnight."

Katie soon had climbed the steep, creaky stairs to the two upstairs bedrooms. She cracked open the door to ten-year-old Alex's cubbyhole of a room. Alex lay on his cot, snoring with his mouth open. On the floor beside him, a huge brown dog looked up guiltily at Katie.

"Some watchdog you are, Little Mike," she whispered. His feathery tail thumped the floor. In her own room, Katie tiptoed over to five-year-old Hannah's bed. Hannah had pushed her covers back and lay curled in a little ball. Her tangled brown curls lay across her face. Katie smoothed the curls back and pulled the quilt up around her little sister.

Without turning on a light, she glanced in the mirror over their dresser. A thin-faced thirteen-year-old girl with a sharp-pointed nose and fly-away, dark hair looked back at her. Katie sighed. No changes here.

Stripping off her sweater and jeans, she tugged on her big nightshirt and climbed into bed. Glancing over at a peacefully sleeping Hannah, she couldn't help getting a lump in her throat.

She remembered how sick Hannah had been when they were staying in a tent at Lonesome Bend Campground. If it hadn't been for a nosy, interfering lady named Phoebe Phillips letting them live in her basement apartment and taking Hannah to the doctor, her little sister might not be here tonight.

"Please, God," prayed Katie. "Take care of Phoebe and help her to heal like new—no matter how crabby and selfish she is sometimes."

Chapter Two

A pale sun was shining in her face when Katie woke the next morning. "Sunshine! I can't believe it." She sat up in bed and looked across the room, where Hannah was struggling to tie her shoelaces.

"Want me to help you, Hannah?"

"No, thank you. I can do it." Hannah's small fingers struggled. "There! See, Katie? I tied a bow." She proudly thrust out her worn tennis shoe, which was topped with a lopsided bow. "It was very hard, but I learned to do it so I could go to kindergarten."

Katie grinned. "Yeah, we Barneses aren't quitters, are we?" She jumped out of bed and hunted clean clothes from the dresser. Snatching up her shoes, she headed for the bathroom and a hot bath in the old claw-foot tub.

On the way, she paused to rap on Alex's door. A sleepy groan told her he was still in bed. "Come on, Alex, get up," Katie coaxed. "Mom had to work last night, so I'll probably have to get you guys off to school." The only sound she heard in response to her words was a gentle scratching at the door. Katie opened the door and Little Mike strolled out, his tail wagging. "You're gonna be in trouble when Mom finds out this dog slept in your room," Katie warned the breathing lump in the bed.

Fifteen minutes later, still combing her damp hair, Katie went downstairs and into the kitchen. To her surprise, Mom was sitting at the kitchen table, reading her Bible and drinking a morning cup of coffee.

"Mom, I thought you'd still be in bed after working last night," Katie said.

"I have too much to do today," her mother answered. "Anyway, I was home in bed by two-thirty. If I get tired, I'll take a nap while you kids are at school." She took a sip of coffee and closed her Bible.

"Did Dad tell you about Phoebe Phillips's car accident last night?" Katie asked, reaching for the bright yellow Cheerios box.

"Yes, wasn't that terrible? I called the hospital early this morning before your dad left for work. Phoebe's still there. She has a broken leg!"

"A broken leg? Wow! Well, we knew she was hurt pretty bad when we saw the medics carry her away on a stretcher. And her car is a total mess." Katie poured a heaping bowl of round little O's and added two spoonfuls of sugar. "But Phoebe was still able to talk. She was screaming at the truck driver and blaming him after she drove right in front of him." Katie poured on some milk and took a mouthful of cereal. "I guess I feel a little guilty, Mom, because I was glad Phoebe wouldn't be able to talk the church trustees into vetoing the homeless shelter last night. Wouldn't that have been just awful?"

"Now, Katie, we have to remember that Phoebe is a caring

Stormy Fall

Christian. She cares about homeless people, too." Mom smiled. "We're living proof of that, aren't we? Let's just pray to God that she'll have a change of mind about Good Samaritan House." Mom stood up. "And now it's time for me to get Hannah and Alex ready for school, and time for you to catch the school bus, young lady."

By the time the bus pulled up at Ben Franklin Junior High that morning, a misty fog was already rolling in, blocking out the sun.

"I don't like this fog much," said Alisha as they all left the bus and trooped into the huge brick school building. "But I do like it better than rain twenty-four hours a day."

"Not me," grumbled Katie. She watched the dim figures of fellow students scurrying toward the school doors. "In this fog you can't tell who's your friend and who isn't."

Alisha stepped forward and swung a heavy plate-glass door open. She looked down the hall toward the rows of lockers, then grinned back at Katie. "Well, here comes one of your friends now, Katie. See you later."

"Oh, no," muttered Katie. "It has to be . . ." She followed Alisha through the door. "Hi, Gwen."

"Well hi, Katie. I thought your bus would never get here." A petite blond girl with shoulder-length curls strolled up to Katie. Gwen Van Switt wore a stunning beige sweater that was the exact shade of her hair. "Isn't it just the most terrible thing about poor Phoebe? When Aunt Berniece heard the news last night, she cried and cried. They're best friends, you know."

"Oh, I know," said Katie. "Yeah, the accident was terrible, all right. It was even more horrible for all of us who saw it. We watched Phoebe being loaded into an ambulance on a stretcher. But where were you, Gwen?"

Gwen smiled as she smoothed her curls. "Aunt Berniece took Nickie and me into Seattle to buy new winter coats at Nordstrom's." She glanced at her beige sweater. "I got this sweater last night, too. Do you like it, Katie?"

Katie shrugged. "Sure, just like your other fifty or so sweaters."

"Oh, Katie," said Gwen with a tinkling little laugh. "You're so silly. I worry about you, though. You always look so cold in that old windbreaker. You need to buy a warm winter jacket, too."

"Oh, don't worry about me." Katie stopped at her locker and stashed the windbreaker and her heavy backpack. "I plan to buy a new jacket real soon." She didn't mention that she had no idea where the money would come from.

"Maybe if your family had stayed in Phoebe's little apartment, *she* would have bought you a new jacket." Gwen laid her hand on Katie's arm. "I really wish you were still staying there, Katie. Aunt Berniece and Mother like my friends to live near me." Gwen scrunched up her nose in a way she thought was cute. Katie thought she looked like a rabbit. "You're still my friend, but, like, we can't see much of each other when you live clear down there in Lower Mapleton."

"You make it sound as if I live in Siberia, Gwen."

Katie closed her locker and tried to walk away, but Gwen stuck like a leech.

"Don't you wish the cheerleaders would hurry up and pick

their new squad members?" she asked. "And won't it be just too, too cool if we both get picked?"

"They're only going to vote in two new cheerleaders," warned Katie.

"I know. And I'll keep my fingers crossed that you'll be one of them." Gwen turned toward the art room and wiggled her fingers. "Bye-bye, Katie."

"Bye." Katie watched Gwen sweep into the art room. Was Gwen really that dense? She really thought she was going to be picked as a cheerleader! Why, she didn't know a single cheerleading routine. In fact, she had spent most of the try-out time worrying about her hair getting messed up.

Katie had first met Gwen last summer, when both their families were camped at Puget Sound State Park. The relationship had never been anything but misery for Katie. When she discovered they would be neighbors while the Barneses were staying at Phoebe's house, Katie felt doomed to a lifetime of being bugged by a girl she really didn't want to know.

It was easy to feel sorry for Gwen. Her dad had abandoned her and her mom. Her mother was an alcoholic. And they had to live with Gwen's stuck-up aunt and cousin. Katie sighed as she turned into the Life Skills room. It was sure easier to feel sorry for Gwen than it was to like her.

After leaving Gwen it was a relief for Katie to begin a new day of classes. She sat down at her table and started worrying about make-believe budgets and new recipes. Her cooking partner, Liz, was already waiting, her hands folded on a bulging brown spiral notebook and a small scowl on her face.

"Wouldn't you know," she complained. "I've worked for

days on my life-skills notebook, and now Mrs. Carter says she won't be collecting them for another week."

Katie stared. "You mean our notebooks were due today? I completely forgot to do mine."

Liz closed her eyes and shook her head. "Oh, Katie, everything turns out good for you, doesn't it?"

As the day went on, Katie began to think Liz had been right. First, Mr. Martin gave her a B+ on the pop quiz she'd taken the day before in social studies class. Then on the bus ride home that afternoon, Alisha reminded her that the next day, Friday, was a teachers' workshop and there wouldn't be any school.

"Which reminds me," Alisha said. "Do you have anything going on tomorrow, Katie?"

"No," Katie admitted.

"Then do you want to go to the Seattle Center with Janie, my mom, and me tomorrow?" asked Alisha. "My mom even said that if she has enough money, we can all ride up those awesome glass elevators to the top of the Space Needle!"

"That sounds great!" Katie said. "I've been dying to see the Space Needle up close."

"All right! We're going to have so much fun, Katie!"

Katie was sure they would. When she got off the school bus, she almost danced down the driveway to her house. But she stopped when she saw her ten-year-old brother, Alex, sitting on the porch looking like he'd lost his last friend. Little Mike lay beside him, gazing sadly up at his beloved master.

"What's wrong, Alex?"

Alex tossed pebbles at a clump of dry grass. "Aw, I hate living here in Mapleton. I just wish we could go back home to Kansas."

"What? Aren't you the kid who was so crazy to move into this old house? You thought it was perfect."

"Yeah, this place is fine. But all the guys in my room at school live up on the hill. And they make fun of me all the time 'cause we're poor. Do you know I'm the only kid in my class who has a black-and-white TV? And no computer! Why can't we get a computer?"

"You know we can't afford a computer right now, Alex. Not 'til we get our debts paid off." Katie laid a hand on Alex's heavy shoulder. "Listen, Alex, maybe Saturday afternoon you and I'll walk over to the library. They've got computers you can use."

Alex shrugged off her hand. "It's not the same."

Katie sighed. "Then maybe you better remember how much better off we are than we were last summer. We've got a home now. Mom and Dad both have jobs. And you've got that new dog you wanted so bad." She grinned down at her brother. "Besides all that, there's no school tomorrow. Life's not all *that* bad here in Mapleton, is it?"

Alex looked up at her and scowled. "You don't think so? Well, just wait 'til you go in the house, Katie."

"Why? What's going on in the house?"

"You'll see." Alex's scowl turned into a grin.

Katie pushed past him and opened the front door. "Mom, I'm home!"

Mom came hurrying from the kitchen, wiping her hands on a towel. "Oh, good, Katie. Something came up, and—"

But Katie was staring at the small suitcase that was sitting near the door. "Who's going away?" she interrupted her mother.

"Well, you see, dear, I called Ellison Simms to ask how Phoebe's doing. He said she's going home this afternoon."

"So? What's that got to do with my suitcase being out here?"

"Phoebe's going to need someone to stay with her for a few days. I'd go, but I have to work nights. Then I remembered there's no school tomorrow because of teachers' workshop. So I thought maybe you'd like to help Phoebe by staying with her over the weekend."

Panic stabbed Katie. "Mom, I can't go to Phoebe's! Alisha just invited me to go to Seattle with her tomorrow! We might even get to go up the Space Needle!"

"Oh, dear," said her mother. "Well, that certainly makes things more difficult. If I had more seniority at the café, I'd take those two days off and go to Phoebe's myself. She's done so much for us."

"Yes, she has," agreed Katie. "But don't forget how hard she worked us when we were staying there, Mom. Besides, Phoebe's got plenty of money. Why can't she hire a private nurse?"

"Oh, she's already hired a nurse. But you know Phoebe. She's a little hard to get along with. Ellison and I thought it'd be good to have someone else there, too, to just help things go smoothly for a few days."

"Are you saying I *have* to go, Mom?" Katie squeaked.

"Of course not. It's up to you, Katie."

"Good. Then I'm staying right here and going to the Seattle Center with my friends tomorrow." Katie slipped off her backpack, crossed the living room, and started upstairs toward her bedroom.

Stormy Fall

"Oh, by the way, Phoebe did say she'd pay you fifty dollars for staying three days," Mom called after her.

Katie stopped. "Fifty dollars?"

"Yep." Mom smiled.

Katie took a deep breath and started figuring. That fifty dollars could buy her a new winter jacket. She stood on the stair step for a minute, then turned and headed back down the stairs. "Okay, Mom, I'll do it. I guess I can stand to stay with Phoebe for three days—I really could use a new jacket." She shrugged off her old windbreaker and started for the closet. "What time will I have to go tomorrow?"

"Ha!" Alex had come in the house behind her and stood there smiling. "Why do you think your suitcase is already packed and waiting?"

"You mean I have to go right now?"

"Certainly not." Mom frowned at Alex. "I'm fixing a really special supper tonight. Your favorite, chicken and dumplings, Katie. And apple crisp for dessert. Then Dad'll drive you up to Phoebe's house. Now, you should go call Alisha and tell her you've had a change in plans."

"Hey, don't look so sour, Katie," Alex said. "Man, I'd even stay with Phoebe for fifty bucks."

Katie didn't bother to reply as she started up the stairs. *Liz was wrong in Lifeskills class today,* she thought glumly. *Things don't always go good for Katie Barnes. And when they go bad, they go* really *bad. But . . . I do need the money.*

When Dad drove Katie up the hill that evening, he didn't even mention the ordeal facing Katie. Instead, he told funny stories about his construction job. "It's not much like farming, or even the factory job I had back home, but I guess we all have to face changes, don't we, Katie."

"That's for sure," sighed Katie.

All too soon they came to the large, well-tended yards and big expensive houses of Phoebe's neighborhood. The brown van turned onto the tree-lined driveway and they drove up to the huge white house with pillars in front.

"I can go in by myself, Dad." Katie reached for her small suitcase, but Dad insisted on walking right up to the front door with her.

A middle-aged woman wearing a starched white uniform answered the doorbell. "Why, you must be Katie." She smiled. "I'm Mrs. Fish, the nurse. Welcome." She took Katie's suitcase from Dad. They talked for a minute and then Katie watched her dad walk away. She wanted to call after him and have him grab her hand in his, like when she was a little kid, and take her back home.

"Come on in, Katie," said Mrs. Fish. "You and I can keep each other's spirits up this weekend."

Katie knew just what she meant as they walked down the broad hallway.

"Mrs. Fish! Mrs. Fish!" called a shrill voice. "Is that girl here yet?"

The kindly nurse raised her eyebrows at Katie. "She just this minute arrived, Mrs. Phillips." She led Kate down the long, plushly carpeted hallway. Phoebe's bedroom was as big as two or three bedrooms in most homes. Phoebe was sitting in a wheelchair near a canopied, king-sized bed. Her left leg was propped up on a cream-colored leather hassock. The leg was in a cast from her ankle to her knee.

"Mrs. Phillips, I'm really sorry about your accident," said Katie.

"Well, of course you are!" snapped Phoebe. "Now take off that dreadful jacket and help me!"

Katie's pity for the old woman was wiped away like old chalk off a chalkboard. This was a weekend that would feel like a week.

Chapter Three

"Come on, dear, I'll show you the room where you'll be sleeping," said Nurse Fish.

From the minute Katie put her jacket and suitcase down in a spare bedroom until eleven that night, she hardly had time to blink an eye. She smoothed a cushion behind Phoebe's rigidly straight back. She picked up things that were dropped. She watered plants. She carried a tray to the kitchen. She fetched a cup of hot herbal tea. She answered the phone four times. At last Nurse Fish insisted that Phoebe go to bed and turn out her light.

Katie dragged her feet to the spare room. Wearily, she changed into her pajamas and climbed into a strange bed. She had barely had time to drop her head onto the pillow and close her eyes when there was a gentle tap at the door.

Mrs. Fish looked in. "I'm so sorry, Katie, but Phoebe can't sleep."

"But what can I do about that?" asked Katie groggily.

Mrs. Fish cleared her throat. "She . . . er, she wants you to read to her for a while out of Psalms."

"I guess I can read her a psalm or two," Katie said.

"Uh, well, she actually requested that you read her the whole book of Psalms."

When Katie managed to open her eyes Friday morning, she moaned. To her surprise, the moan came out a raspy whisper. "Great. Thanks to Phoebe, I've lost my voice," she croaked. It had taken seventy-one psalms to put the stubborn patient to sleep.

There was a tap at the bedroom door and Nurse Fish walked in. "'Morning, Katie." She brought Katie a tray of breakfast—hot cereal, a soft-boiled egg, and orange juice.

Katie slid out of bed and took the tray. "Mrs. Fish, *you're* the nurse," she rasped. "You don't have to wait on me."

"Honey, you deserve it after last night. And I've got something in my bag that'll help that throat."

The nurse was back soon with a package of throat lozenges. "Take one of these after you've eaten breakfast." She looked at the tray. "And you'd better eat everything, Katie. You've got one busy day ahead of you."

She sat in a rocking chair while Katie ate. "I've known Phoebe Phillips nearly my whole life," she said. "We went through school together." Mrs. Fish rocked silently for a minute. "Phoebe hasn't changed a bit. She's always thought she was a little better than the rest of us and she figures she knows more than anyone else." The kindly nurse laughed. "Funny, though, for all that, I never could help liking her."

She stood up. "Well now, you and I are working folks, Katie. We'd better get busy."

Friday was like a repeat of Thursday evening—except there was more of it. After breakfast and a throat lozenge Katie answered more phone calls in a raspy voice, made more cups of herbal tea, and ran up and down stairs like a robot. Then there was the doorbell and all of Phoebe's friends who dropped in. Those who could not come in person had flowers delivered.

Pastor Miller made a hurried visit before lunch. He brought a big, rust-colored chrysanthemum plant from the church. As he was leaving, he stopped to chat with Katie. "This is a fine Christian thing you're doing, Katie, helping Phoebe in her hour of need. We're all proud—"

"Katie!" called a shrill voice from Phoebe's room. "Come in here at once! I need you!"

Katie clamped her lips together to keep from telling her pastor she would never be spending three days waiting on this selfish woman if it were not for the fifty dollars. She turned and went into Phoebe's room.

"The phone! Didn't you hear the phone ringing?" shrieked Phoebe.

"But, look—if you just pushed your wheelchair a few inches, you could reach it yourself," Katie said.

Phoebe gasped. "Katie! Don't you have any compassion for the injured? Answer the phone, young lady!"

Katie picked up the phone. "Phillips's residence." She listened and then turned to Phoebe. "It's your cousin, Ellison Simms. He wants to stop by and see you after lunch."

Phoebe's scowl changed into a wide, sunny smile. "Oh, by all means. The dear boy. How thoughtful—taking time out from his busy day at the flower shop to visit his old cousin."

After she completed the call and hung up the phone, Katie was busier than ever, picking up and dusting and seeing that everything in the spotless bedroom was perfect. Mrs. Fish changed her patient into another expensive robe and fixed her hair for her.

At one o'clock on the dot, Mrs. Fish answered the door and led a tall, pale-skinned man in a dark suit into his cousin's room. He was carrying an enormous bouquet of pink roses.

"Now, that fellow I never did care for," Mrs. Fish told Katie when she came out. "He's always been shifty-eyed, even as a little kid." Katie laughed.

There was a stream of visitors that Friday afternoon, including Phoebe's best friend, Berniece Stimson, and her daughter, Nichole, Gwen Van Switt's aunt and cousin. Katie looked out to see if Gwen were following behind them.

"Gwen's not coming?" she asked.

"Why, no, she's staying home with her sick mother." Berniece looked hard at Katie for a minute. Slowly she began taking off her luxurious fur coat. "Here, my dear, you may put this away in the hall closet." She laid the silky-feeling coat over Katie's arm. "And by the way . . . Katie, isn't it? I realize you and my niece were friends while you were staying with Phoebe this summer. But that must change now, of course. The two of you would have nothing in common now that you're living in Lower Mapleton."

Mrs. Stimson turned to her daughter. "Come, Nichole, let's go see dear Phoebe."

"Just a minute, Mother." Nichole paused to remove her expensive suede jacket, laying it in Katie's arms with a smile. Then she followed her mother into Phoebe's bedroom.

Mrs. Fish watched the two of them go, then arched her eyebrows at Katie.

Katie started toward the hall closet. "I've never cared much

Stormy Fall

for those two, either," Katie said, a grim look on her face. "They keep their noses too high in the air." She and Mrs. Fish both laughed again.

At dinnertime, when Katie carried in Phoebe's tray, Phoebe looked at her suspiciously. "Katie, are you coming down with something? You sound hoarse. I don't want to catch anything."

"It's because of all that reading from the Psalms that she did for you last night, Phoebe," said Nurse Fish, who had come in behind Katie.

"Hmm. Well, that was a good deal of reading. I don't think we'll do that again tonight." Phoebe took time to bow her head in a silent prayer of thanks for the food. "Amen," she said. She turned back to Katie. "No, Katie, I believe we'll read from the book of Romans instead tonight."

But Katie didn't have to read that night after all. Nurse Fish decided that Phoebe had overdone it on her first day home. She gave her a good rubdown and sat beside her until she fell asleep. The door was hardly closed before Katie heard the sound of ladylike snores.

Saturday started out as a quiet day. While Mrs. Fish was giving Phoebe a sponge bath, Katie found time to call home for the first time. Mom was very sympathetic.

"Oh, Katie, you sound really bad. Why don't I come and take your place today and tomorrow?"

"No, that's okay," Katie said. "My voice is doing better than it was yesterday. I've earned half of that fifty dollars already. I can last another day and a half."

"Are you sure?" Mom said.

"Positive."

But right before lunchtime, the dishwasher quit working.

Stormy Fall

"There's going to be a short delay for lunch, Phoebe," Mrs. Fish said. "I'll have to wash the dishes and pans by hand before I can fix a meal."

"Nonsense!" said Phoebe. "Katie can wash those dishes."

"No, no, that's quite all right," Mrs. Fish protested. "I'll do it. The dishwasher's nearly filled with dirty dishes and pans."

Phoebe sat up very erect in her wheelchair. "Gilda Fish, did you graduate with honors from nursing school so you could wash my dishes? I said Katie will do it. She might as well do *something* to earn that fifty dollars."

Katie thought at that moment that she would probably never, ever be able to have Christian love for Phoebe Phillips. After washing dishes and pans for an hour and a half, she was even more certain.

Katie looked at the kitchen phone many times. Should she call Mom? Her mother would gladly take her place this weekend. But she couldn't. "I started this job," she whispered over the stack of greasy pots and pans. "I'll finish it."

The disturbing phone call came at early evening. "Phillips's residence." Katie held the phone in her red, wrinkly "dishpan" hands. She turned to Phoebe. "It's your cousin Mr. Simms again. He says he wants to talk to you personally."

Phoebe snatched the phone and pressed it to her ear. "Ellison, dear, what is it? . . . What's that you're saying? No—it can't be!" She motioned for Katie to leave the room and shut the door. "They wouldn't dare! This is totally unacceptable!" Her words came right through the heavy wooden door as if it was paper.

Nurse Fish came running down the hall. "What's going on? I heard Phoebe hollering clear down in the kitchen."

"I don't know. It was only a phone call from her cousin," Katie said in dismay.

"My goodness, it must have been terrible news." Mrs. Fish and Katie both stared at the closed door. The last sound they heard was the slamming down of the telephone. Then everything was quiet. Nurse Fish had her hand on the doorknob when Phoebe called out.

"Gilda! Katie! Come in here!"

They both dashed for the door.

Phoebe's face was as white as that of a painted circus clown. There was a tiny red spot of color high on each cheek. "I have had some shocking news." She reached for a tissue and blew her nose. "My dear cousin, Ellison, told me . . ." She stopped and ripped the tissue in half. "He told me the church trustees had their meeting last night without me." The red spots on her cheeks had grown bigger. "They voted one hundred percent to turn Ms. Foster's house into a shelter for homeless people!"

"Well, Phoebe," said Mrs. Fish, "that sounds good to me. There are a lot of homeless folks around, and winter's coming. I know you're concerned about them, too."

"Concerned?" said Phoebe. "Well . . . well of course I'm concerned! I'm an enormous contributor to Seattle Union Mission." She looked over at Katie. "Why, sometimes I've even trusted homeless families to live in my basement apartment!" Katie felt her face grow hot. Why couldn't people just let that story die?

"But this!" continued Phoebe, pounding the arm of her chair with her fist. "This is something else altogether. We would be allowing dirty men and . . . and bag ladies to live

Stormy Fall

beside our church when we know nothing about them. Who knows what they might do or steal? Why, they could attend our church services and steal from the collection plate if they felt so inclined!" Phoebe's long face twisted like a little kid who wanted to cry. "I had hoped to sell that old house and buy beautiful stained-glass windows for the church. We might even have some money left over to send to the mission." A tear streaked down her face.

Finally, she turned and looked from Katie to Mrs. Fish. "I have made up my mind," she announced. "Both of you plan to get up early tomorrow morning. We are going to church!"

"Oh, no, Phoebe, that's not a good idea. You know the doctor told you to stay home through the weekend." The nurse took Phoebe's bony wrist and began to check her pulse.

"Nonsense!" Phoebe pulled her arm free. "I said we are going to church! I must talk to my friends and Pastor Miller about this disgrace. When the congregation sees me wheeled down the aisle with this broken leg . . ."—her voice began to quiver—"oh, those trustees will regret what they have done!"

"But Mrs. Phillips," said Katie. "You don't have a car anymore, remember? Your car is at the wrecking yard."

"Well . . ." For the first time Phoebe looked like she didn't know what to do. Then she turned to Mrs. Fish. "You have a car, don't you, Gilda?"

"Yes, my old Ford station wagon."

"Fine. We will drive to the church in your car. Now, Katie, if you will bring my dinner tray, I'm suddenly feeling famished."

Stormy Fall

On Sunday morning, after a long struggle, Mrs. Fish and Katie managed to get both Phoebe and the wheelchair into the station wagon. The old wagon coughed and choked, then rumbled down the long driveway. The loose right front fender rattled merrily.

Phoebe's face was red. "I rather hope not too many people will see us arrive," she said.

Nurse Fish chuckled. "By the time we get you and that wheelchair out of my car, Phoebe, I'm certain all of the church people will be inside." She drove slowly and carefully down the road and into the church parking lot.

The station wagon glided to a stop in front of the church entrance. Mrs. Fish and Katie jumped out and began to struggle with the wheelchair. Luckily, two men spied them and came to their aid. Within minutes, Phoebe and her wheelchair were sitting in the entry to the sanctuary.

"Thank you. We can handle this now," Nurse Fish told the men quietly.

"Wait!" whispered Katie as the organ thundered out and the singing began. "Maybe we should stay here until this song ends."

"Nonsense!" snapped Phoebe. "You wheel me right down there to my regular pew beside Ellison."

"Just a minute there, ladies!" Two small, shabbily dressed women who had been sitting in a back pew hurried up to them. "Let us push you!" Edith and Stella Tootle jerked the wheelchair from Mrs. Fish.

"Stop! Stop, you—you—" gasped Phoebe. At that instant the hymn ended and the organ stopped.

"Remove your hands from my wheelchair!" commanded

Stormy Fall

Phoebe. Her long, thin face turned red as she saw every pair of eyes in the auditorium watching them. Every pair of ears was tuned in to her words.

Katie thought she'd die from shame. Could she ever live this down? She was thankful her family didn't seem to be there. They must have attended the early service today.

The Tootle sisters pulled to a stop. "Why, we just wanted to help, Mrs. Phillips." Edith patted Phoebe's shoulder with a hand that wasn't quite clean; dirt was clearly visible under Edith's fingernails. "We were looking for a good deed to do. And you, sister, looked like you could use it. You see, the pastor tells us we get to be the first ones to live in the Good Samaritan home." Bending down, she smiled into Phoebe's horrified face.

Phoebe Phillips made a little squeaking sound and fainted dead away.

Chapter Four

The church looked like a busy anthill. Two men in dark suits rushed up and took the Tootle sisters back to their seats. Ellison Simms dashed in with a glass of water and soon revived Phoebe from her faint. Phoebe's friends scurried over from all sides to check on her. Berniece Stimson began fanning Phoebe's pale face with a church bulletin.

"Let me through, please!" Nurse Fish pushed her way through to Phoebe and began taking her pulse. She nodded and smiled. "Mrs. Phillips is going to be just fine, folks. You can all go back to your seats now."

The choir director turned and began wildly waving his arms. At last the choir members paid attention and began to sing. "Praise God from whom all blessings flow. . . ."

One by one, people slowly returned to their seats. Katie and Mrs. Fish took the two nearest empty seats. Phoebe's wheelchair was scooted up beside them. *If I could,* thought Katie, *I'd hide under this pew and not come out until the church building is empty.*

But the rousing service perked Phoebe up; by the closing hymn, rosy color had come back to her long face. As Mrs. Fish slowly shoved the wheelchair down the aisle, Phoebe nodded and smiled weakly at her friends.

Stormy Fall

Katie looked around when she felt someone tap her shoulder. "Alisha!"

"Oh, Katie," Alisha whispered, "we missed you so much Friday. Was your weekend at Phoebe's as awful as I think it must have been?"

Katie rolled her eyes. "The worst weekend of my entire life," she whispered back. "It all started—" She broke off abruptly. "Uh-oh."

". . . And let me tell you something else, Philip Brown!" screeched an angry voice ahead of them. Phoebe was speaking for the first time since her fainting spell, each word coming louder than the last.

"I have to go, Alisha," Katie said. "Phoebe's cornered another of the trustees. If we don't get her in the car soon, there's no telling what she might do to the poor man."

But Nurse Fish was a pro with problem patients. Within fifteen minutes Phoebe was snugly belted into the front passenger seat of the station wagon. Her wheelchair was stowed in the back, and the three of them were ready to go.

As they left the parking lot, the nurse glanced over at her patient. "All in all, that really was a wonderful service today. Don't you think so, Phoebe?"

"Wonderful?" Phoebe's voice wobbled. "Gilda, this has been the most humiliating morning of my life. I have never felt so degraded!"

"Now, dear, I'm sure no one meant to embarrass you." Nurse Fish looked back. "Don't you agree, Katie?"

"Oh, yes," replied Katie. "In fact, the Tootle sisters are really very nice ladies when you get to know them."

"Ladies!" Phoebe snorted. "Those two loud, uncouth old

Stormy Fall

women must never be allowed to disrupt another service at our church! This terrible fiasco is simply proof that we should never put a shelter for people like them next to our beautiful church building. Never!" She was so upset, the threats sprayed from her mouth. "No matter what I have to do to stop it!"

"Why, Phoebe Phillips," scolded Mrs. Fish. "You shouldn't say things like that. Some people might think they sounded like a threat."

Katie didn't speak. She was busy praying. "Please, God, change Phoebe's mind," she whispered. "Don't let her ruin Edith and Stella's lives."

Even "the worst weekend of my entire life" finally came to an end for Katie. She was actually humming as she packed her suitcase to go home on Sunday evening.

Phoebe looked disappointed when Katie came into her room carrying the suitcase. "You're leaving already, Katie? But you didn't get my get-well cards pasted into a scrapbook."

"Sorry," said Katie hoarsely. "Uh, could I have the fifty dollars now, please?"

"On Sunday? Why, Katie, I don't do business on Sunday. Just run along home if you must. I'll get the money to you soon." Phoebe sighed loudly. "Gilda, I do believe I'll let you put me to bed now. I'm feeling weary."

Forlornly, Katie went to stand by a window and watch for her family. They were picking her up after the Sunday evening service. The minute she saw the van turning into Phoebe's driveway, she ran out to meet them.

"I was hoping to come in and visit with Phoebe for a minute," Mom said.

"She's already in bed," replied Katie. She slid open the back door and scrambled into the van. "Let's go!"

"Oh, Daddy, could we drive out back and see where we used to live?" begged Hannah.

Dad chuckled as he slowly drove around to the backyard. He stopped in front of the basement apartment of Phoebe's huge house. "There it is, Hannah. Our home for several weeks—when we really needed it."

"Thanks to the good Lord and Phoebe Phillips," Mom added.

The dark windows of the apartment looked cold and unfriendly. Katie shivered. "It makes that old house of ours look pretty good, doesn't it? Can we go, please?"

As the van moved out onto the road, Alex leaned over Katie's seat back. "Hey, Katie, let me see your fifty bucks."

"I didn't get it tonight," Katie said glumly. "Phoebe said she doesn't do business on Sunday."

"Yeah, I'll bet that's just an excuse," jeered Alex. "You probably won't ever get your money from the old tightwad."

"Alex!" snapped Mom. "That's enough from you. Of course Katie will get the money. I told Phoebe she needs it to buy a winter coat." Mom smiled back at Katie. "The important thing is that you helped someone in their time of need. We're proud of you."

But that won't keep me warm and dry this winter, thought Katie. She stared out the car window into the black night.

Katie slept soundly in her own bed Sunday night. Monday morning, she looked out the window and saw that a light rain was sleepily drifting down onto the world. Katie didn't care. She threw back her quilt, jumped out of bed, and danced over to the dresser.

Stormy Fall

"Good morning, Katie Barnes!" she said to her reflection. A happy-faced girl with a pointed nose grinned back at her. "I'm not hoarse anymore!" she sang out.

When she bounced down the stairs to breakfast that morning, the whole family was sitting around the table waiting for her.

"Dad doesn't have to be at work until nine this morning, so since you're back home, we figured we'd all eat together," Mom said.

"Why don't you say the prayer, Katie?" Dad said.

"Sure." Katie looked around the table at each familiar face. She bowed her head. "Boy, am I glad to be back home, Lord," she began. Then she prayed for God's blessing on the food.

"It sure is good to have our family together again," Dad said when she had finished.

"Absolutely," Mom added. "I heard Phoebe was pretty upset at the second service yesterday," she said as she buttered her toast.

Katie nodded. "It was terrible. Poor Edith and Stella just wanted to help, and Phoebe acted like they had leprosy. Everyone was watching us."

Dad laughed. "Phoebe doesn't mean everything she says. You might say her bark's worse than her bite."

"Oh, she meant everything she said, Dad." Katie paused to swallow a bite of oatmeal. "Phoebe Phillips *does* hate poor homeless people. Especially now that the other trustees voted to approve Good Samaritan House." She shrugged. "Anyway, I'm praying that she'll change her mind. And God still does miracles, doesn't He?"

"Every single day," Dad said. He looked up at the clock.

"And if I don't get to work pretty soon, it may take a miracle to keep that job of mine."

"And I've got a school bus coming in a few minutes," said Katie. She daubed some blackberry jam on her piece of toast and ate it as she hurried upstairs.

When she came back down, Mom was still sitting at the table with a pile of recipes spread out in front of her. Dad had already left for work.

"So, what are you planning on cooking, Mom?" asked Katie.

"Oh, something really special for the big Harvest Dinner at church Saturday night." Mom picked up a recipe card. "I think I may make Grandma Ross's sweet-potato casserole."

"Yummy! I love that!" Katie snatched up her lunch sack and started out the back door. "Bye, Mom!" She dashed through the misty rain to meet the school bus.

There was more talk about the Harvest Dinner on the bus that morning. Tim and Shad sat behind Katie and Alisha. Tim poked Katie. "Hey, you two, be sure to come to the youth meeting Wednesday night. The junior high kids are in charge of serving at the Harvest Dinner this year. We've gotta plan it."

"What's so special about this Harvest Dinner?" Katie said. "Mom had recipes spread all over the table this morning."

"It's the church's fall missionary project," Tim said.

"And the best eating, for sure," Mark Gomez said from his spot behind Tim. "Everybody brings tons of their special food, and we all eat 'til we're stuffed. I can hardly wait!" Mark rubbed his stomach.

"It's always held on the first Saturday night in November, and half the town of Mapleton comes," said Alisha.

"You see, there's no set cost for the meal—everyone gives

whatever they feel like giving. And a lot of people feel extra generous after all that food," added Tim.

"Yeah," Shad said. "Last year, Pastor Miller put two big aluminum dishpans in the middle of the table. He challenged everyone there to help fill them with cash. They collected almost two thousand dollars."

"We hope to pass that this year," Tim said. "The money will be used to fix up Good Sam House."

"Awesome!" Katie said.

"Okay, you guys, shut up and let us have some girl talk," Alisha said, motioning for the boys to sit back. She turned to Katie. "Now. Tell me everything about your weekend."

"Well, it was a weekend I'll never forget," Katie said with a grimace. "No matter how much I'd like to." She was still telling her story when their bus pulled up at the school.

"I'll bet there's not one other girl in the church who would've stayed for three days with Phoebe Phillips," Alisha said as they climbed off the bus. "You've got guts, Katie."

Katie shrugged modestly. "I guess I've always had a lot of nerve." She turned toward the lockers. "Besides, there was the fifty dollars."

Gwen Van Switt, dressed in matching green sweater and skirt, came by as Katie opened her locker. "Oh, Katie, I'm so sorry I couldn't come over to Phoebe's house Saturday while you were there."

Katie hung her windbreaker and put her lunch on the shelf. "Your aunt said your mom was sick. Sorry to hear that, Gwen. How's she doing today?"

"Oh, Mommy's just great today. She had a bad headache Saturday, but now everything's wonderful."

Stormy Fall

There was something weird about Gwen's voice. Katie had been taking books from her backpack, but she turned to look up into Gwen's baby-blue eyes. "Really?"

The blond girl nodded her head up and down, but her lip quivered and a tear rolled down her cheek. "All right, you want the truth?" she said angrily. "Mommy's not fine. She's an alcoholic, and she lost her job as a receptionist Friday because she was d-drunk! There! Are you happy now, Katie?"

"I—no, of course I'm not happy," Katie answered. "But at least you're being honest, Gwen. I'll pray for your mom if you'd like."

"Oh, save your prayers," Gwen said. "I hardly think the Van Switts need someone to pray for them who lives in an old shack in Lower Mapleton." Then Gwen turned on her heel and hurried away.

Katie turned away too, fury boiling inside her. *I'm glad the two of us aren't friends,* she thought. *I couldn't stand to be friends with someone who could make me so mad!*

Before she disappeared into the crowd, Gwen looked back. "Don't you tell anyone what I told you, Katie. I don't want kids to talk about me."

"Don't worry!" snapped Katie. She turned away from Gwen and didn't look back.

The big talk at the next midweek youth meeting was not about Mrs. Van Switt's drinking. It was about the coming Harvest Dinner.

"You'll have to wear a black dress or a black top and long skirt, Katie," Alisha said when Katie walked into the meeting. "Then we'll wear white pilgrim hats and wide white collars."

"I can't do that!" protested Katie. "I'd feel so stupid!"

"Now, Katie, of course you'll do it," said Mrs. Kipper. "Phoebe Phillips wants all the servers to be costumed like pilgrims this year."

"What's Phoebe got to do with this, anyway? She's home in a wheelchair with a broken leg."

Joan Kipper smiled. "Mrs. Phillips is always in charge of the Harvest Dinner. Anyway, she has an electric wheelchair now, and she's getting pretty good at wheeling around in it. She's promised to be at the dinner Saturday night."

"Great." Katie looked over at a row of boys, sitting back with their arms folded and a stubborn set to their mouths. "What about them? Do they have to dress like pilgrims, too?"

"We chickened out," Ed Kipper said. He laughed. "But we had to agree to carry out the dirty dishes and clean up the tables afterward."

"Come on, Katie. It'll be fun," urged Sue Wong. "Trust me, you'll make a cute pilgrim. Besides, this is all to help Good Sam House get started."

Katie held out her hands. "Okay, okay, I'll do it . . . but I won't like it."

"Atta girl," said Sue. "Now, why don't we sit down and get this dinner planning done."

"Sue's cool for an 'on the hill' girl, isn't she?" Alisha whispered to Katie.

"Yeah," Katie whispered back. "She's pretty good at convincing people to do what she says, too. But I'm still going to feel like a dork at the dinner!"

Alisha grinned. "You? What about me? How many black pilgrims do you suppose there were?" They both started giggling.

Chapter Five

*O*n Saturday evening, Katie put on her black knit top and a long black skirt that a neighbor lady had loaned to her. She perched the silly little "pilgrim" hat on her head and posed in front of her bedroom mirror. "Ah, man! I *do* look like a dork!"

"No, you look pretty, Katie." Hannah sat on her bed and gazed up at her big sister. "You'll be the most beautiful pilgrim at the Harvest Dinner."

"Oh, Hannah, every girl ought to have a little sister like you," said Katie. "Now come on. Grab your coat and let's go. Mom and Dad are waiting."

Mom, Dad, and Alex were sitting in the car when the girls came downstairs. The inside of the van was rich with the spicy aroma of Mom's three big sweet-potato casseroles.

"I'm gonna eat 'til I bust tonight," said Alex from the rear seat.

Dad's laugh rumbled out. "Now, Alex, you'd better save a little for the rest of the folks." He inhaled deeply. "I tell you, if all the food tonight smells as good as your mom's sweet-potato casseroles, we're in for a treat."

Little Mike looked forlorn as he sat on the front porch to wait for them to return home.

Alex rolled down a window. "I'll bring you some table scraps tonight, Little Mike," he yelled as the van bumped down the driveway.

It was easy to see that the Harvest Dinner was a popular event in Mapleton. A steady stream of cars were rolling into the church parking lot when the old brown van chugged in.

"It looks like we'll have a record crowd tonight," said Mrs. Reilly, who was parked next to them. She peeped under the foil wrap at one of Mom's sweet-potato casseroles. "My, that looks good, Sarah. I just sent my Tim to the kitchen with four apple pies." She turned and began collecting little Reillys, who were scattering in every direction. "Come here, you!" she said, collaring one of Tim's little brothers.

Mom laughed. "We'll see you as soon as we deliver these casseroles, Maggie."

When Katie got to the church's kitchen door, she stopped, pulled her little white hat from her pocket, and crammed it on her head. She felt better when she saw the other girls awkwardly fingering their own pilgrim hats. Only Gwen Van Switt looked comfortable as she swayed around the kitchen in a silky black dress and white collar. Her cap sat at a perfect angle on her curly blond hair.

"Good evening, ladies!" All the laughing and talking that had been going on came to a halt as if someone had flipped a switch. Every set of eyes watched Phoebe Phillips slowly guide her motorized electric wheelchair into the middle of the crowded kitchen, where she could run everything.

"Alisha Asher! Are you chewing gum while you serve food

Stormy Fall

at our Harvest Dinner?" Phoebe halfway raised herself from her wheelchair. "Don't you girls realize the mayor of Mapleton and his wife are here tonight? We have a reputation to uphold!"

"Sorry, Mrs. Phillips." Alisha rolled her eyes at Katie. She blew one last perfect pink bubble, then tossed her big wad of gum into the nearest trash basket. Katie grinned back at her.

They watched as Phoebe's friend Berniece Stimson placed her hands on Phoebe's bony shoulders. "We're so fortunate you're able to be back managing things again so soon, Phoebe dear."

Phoebe smiled sadly, patting her friend's hand. "It breaks my heart, Berniece, to see the common element seeping into our church to such an extent recently." Her long face brightened. "However, my cousin Ellison has outdone himself with his floral decorations, don't you all agree?"

"Oh, yes. It's wonderful to have Ellison and his lovely flower shop here in Mapleton," gushed Berniece. No one else uttered a word.

"Yes, well, I do hope the congregation realizes how fortunate it is that Ellison agreed to be church treasurer. He knows all there is to know about finances as well as flowers." Phoebe looked around the room as if daring any of the hot, sweaty workers to disagree with her.

"Ellison is twice as expensive as any other florist in town," Katie heard Mrs. Flanagan whisper. "Wouldn't you think he would have donated his flowers tonight?"

"Me, I liked it when we brought garden flowers and decorated the tables ourselves," Mrs. Gomez replied.

"Ready, girls?" One of the kitchen workers held the swinging doors open while the costumed serving girls staggered out with their trays of steaming food.

"Stop right there!" Phoebe snatched at Katie's arm as she started through the doorway. Katie yelped as she almost dropped her heavy tray.

"What is in that blue dish you're carrying, Katie?"

"That blue dish is a platter of my homemade tamales!" Mrs. Gomez said with fire in her eyes.

"Tamales!" Phoebe raised her plucked eyebrows as she looked over at her friend Berniece. Berniece, her mouth in a tight line, nodded in silent agreement. Katie sped out of the kitchen with the tray before they could complain about anything else.

The servers had little time to worry about their costumes as they rushed in and out of the hot, steamy kitchen. It was almost eight o'clock before the girls were able to sit down at a table in the kitchen and eat.

"Wow, there sure is a crowd tonight," said Claudia. "Even the overflow dining room is crammed."

"Isn't it cool?" Sue said. "I wonder how much money we'll have for Good Sam House. Oh, and Katie!" Sue turned to Katie and gave her a warm smile. "Could I talk to you alone for a second?"

"Sure, Sue," Katie said.

"Great." Sue took Katie's arm and led her away from the crowd to the far side of the room. Turning toward Katie, she said, "Katie, you were terrific at the cheerleader tryouts last week."

"Well, thanks." Katie beamed. A compliment from Sue was special. "I was a seventh-grade cheerleader at our middle school in Kansas last year."

Stormy Fall

"Really? I could tell you'd had a lot more experience than the other girls. And you knew all the cheers perfectly."

"Thanks, Sue!" Katie said.

"Well, I just wanted to tell you that," Sue said. "See ya, Katie."

"See ya." Katie stood there as Sue hurried off, feeling like she'd had a warm hug. A curious Alisha hurried over to her. "What was that all about?"

Katie smiled. "Oh, she was just practically telling me I'm gonna be one of the two new cheerleaders. Sue's captain of the squad, you know."

"That's great, Katie!" Alisha's eyes grew big. "You're so brave. I don't think any other Lower Mapleton girl had the nerve to try out for cheerleader."

Katie shrugged. "Well, how are those snobs on the hill gonna know how good we are if we don't show them?"

"Shhh, girls!" Mrs. Flanagan cautioned. "I think the program is ready to start."

The kitchen door swung open once again and Ellison Simms's long face popped in. Not a single light-brown hair was out of place. He beckoned to Phoebe and Berniece. "Phoebe, we're saving seats for you and Berniece at the front table," he said importantly. "I know you want to watch the program."

"I *suppose* I can leave the kitchen workers to handle things by themselves." Phoebe sounded doubtful. Katie saw Mrs. Gomez make a little face at Mrs. Flanagan.

"I can hardly wait for this program," Alisha said. "Our high school youth group planned the music this year. It's gonna be awesome."

Stormy Fall

"I hope we'll have rock music," Claudia said.

But the first song, a duet, was not Christian rock. Instead, it sounded like a song Grandma Ross would have loved.

"Sowing in the morning, sowing seeds of kindness..."

The voices wavered a little but the harmony was good.

"So who's singing?" asked someone in the kitchen.

"It doesn't sound like anyone I know," replied someone else.

"Would you all kindly step aside so I can get in?" Phoebe wheeled herself to the swinging door. "We must have guest singers tonight." Without waiting for Berniece, she pushed open the door and started to wheel herself into the dining hall. She stopped short. The door slammed back against her wheelchair, but Phoebe didn't seem to notice. "No, it can't be!" she cried. "Not again!"

The kitchen crew gasped as she tossed her lap robe aside and tried to stand up. She had taken a clumping step toward the outside door when someone grabbed her and eased her back into the wheelchair.

"I demand that somebody take me home!" shouted Phoebe. But no one made a move to obey. Everyone was too busy cheering and clapping for the two little old ladies with flyaway gray hair and dresses borrowed from the church missionary barrel.

"Why, I didn't even know Stella could talk," said Mrs. Gomez.

"Neither did I," Mrs. Flanagan agreed. "But, praise the Lord, we sure know now she can sing!"

When the whistling and applause had finally died down, the kitchen door swung open one more time. Shad Emery

Stormy Fall

staggered through with a huge tray of dirty dishes. "I think this is the last load," he said. He turned to the table of girls. "Hey, guys! Pastor Miller says for you to come out to the dining hall. The Apostles from Seattle are playing next!"

"Yes!" Alisha dropped her fork. "Come on, Katie!"

The girls all yanked off their little white caps and noisily crowded through the doorway.

Mrs. Emery shook her head, but chuckled. "No use trying to quiet them down now. I reckon when we put those high school kids in charge of a program, you have to expect a little more noise."

Mrs. Gomez answered her, but no one heard a word as the Apostles blasted out their first amplified note.

⌒

On the drive home that night, Katie could hardly keep from bouncing up and down in her seat. "Weren't the Apostles awesome? They're the coolest group I've ever heard!"

"And the loudest," Mom added. "My ears are still ringing! I liked the harpist who played the nice quiet hymns."

"I have to admit I enjoyed it all," Dad said. "Like the Good Book says, we should make a joyful noise unto the Lord."

"Aw, Dad, you just say that because you can't sing," said Alex.

Dad laughed. "I believe you're right, son."

"But you all know who got the most clapping and cheers tonight, don't you?" asked Katie.

"The Tootle sisters!" said Alex, and everyone agreed.

Stormy Fall

"By the way, I didn't see Phoebe after the program," Mom said. "Did she leave early?"

"Right in the middle of Edith and Stella's duet. She got her friend Berniece to wheel her out the back way and take her home." Katie was quiet as she remembered the fury on Phoebe's face. The Tootles made a lot of new friends when they sang tonight, but she was afraid they had made one enemy.

In the darkness of the van, Hannah moved close to Katie. She leaned her head against her big sister's shoulder. Suddenly, she sat up straight. "I smell roast turkey!" She and Katie both looked back at Alex.

"Hey, I'm just taking a few scraps home to Little Mike," Alex said. "He looked so lonesome when we left tonight."

"All those delicious smells tonight reminded me it's time to start planning our own Thanksgiving dinner," Mom said. She looked over at Dad. "I think we can afford a turkey this year, don't you, Harvey?"

"At least a small one," Dad said, chuckling as he carefully drove the van down the foggy road. "It'd be nice if we could still have a house full of company like we always did back home for Thanksgiving."

"Well, I did invite Stella and Edith Tootle," Mom said. "They seem to enjoy being at our place. The poor souls. Imagine spending Thanksgiving in a little motel room."

"Yep, those little ladies are good friends of this family, and I always say we can never have too many friends." Dad shifted the van into a lower gear and slowed as they came to downtown Mapleton.

"Then is it okay if I spend this Sunday night with Skip

Young?" asked Alex. "He's a new friend I made at the dinner. We're in the same room at school, but I hardly talked to him at all before tonight."

"I don't know about that," Mom said slowly. "Skip Young? Let's see, doesn't his family live in one of those new houses up on the other side of the church?"

"Yeah. His mom's dead, so it's just Skip and his brother and their dad. But Skip's really cool. We're gonna work together on a project for social studies."

Mom looked over at Dad again and Katie saw his head nod in agreement. "Well, I'll talk to Skip's dad tomorrow morning, Alex," she said. "If it's okay with him, I guess you can stay tomorrow night."

"Hey, Alex," Katie said. "I thought you were the one who couldn't stand any of the kids who live on the hill."

"Yeah, well, I've decided a few of 'em may be okay."

Katie smiled in the dark. She thought of Sue and the nice things she had said at the dinner that night. "I think you might be right, Alex," she said. "A few of them may be okay."

Chapter Six

"Why does this school bus always smell like sweaty socks and stale peanut-butter sandwiches?" grouched Katie on Monday morning. She took off her heavy backpack and sat down beside Alisha.

"Ha! My Uncle Sean says we 'sissies' oughta be thankful we get to ride to school," said Tim, sitting across the aisle from them. "He says he had to walk the same three miles to and from school when he was a kid. And it was uphill both ways. In the snow. He says we're all softies."

"Softies, huh?" Katie felt the bus start out with a jerk that almost gave her whiplash. She leaned across the aisle. "Your Uncle Sean didn't have Judd Jones for a bus driver," she whispered.

Tim and Shad laughed.

"Would the three of you please be quiet?" pleaded Alisha. "I'm trying to get a little rest so I can ace my English exam first period."

"Rest sounds like a great idea." Katie leaned her head back against the cracked plastic of the bus seat. She closed her eyes as the bus banged over the railroad crossing and churned up the hill.

No one was very talkative that morning. Several kids had

Stormy Fall

their notebooks open, trying to finish homework before they got to school. Even more closed their eyes and tried to grab a last few minutes of sleep before the school day began, or stared out the window without seeing a thing.

Judd Jones noisily shifted gears as the climb up the hill got steeper.

"Katie! Look over at the church building!"

Katie felt Alisha's sharp elbow jabbing her in the side. "Huh? What?"

Alisha excitedly pointed out the bus window. "The church!"

Wide awake now, Katie leaned forward. Her eyes followed Alisha's pointing finger. She gasped as, once again, she saw red and blue flashing lights outside the big brick church building. Official-looking white police cars surrounded the parking lot. "What could have happened this time?"

"Quiet, you two," groaned a sleepy Tim.

"Yeah, give us a break. We need sleep!" Shad said.

Katie reached over and roughly shook Tim's arm. "Look, you guys! Something's going on at the church! Police cars are everywhere!"

By now the bus was a buzz of excited voices.

"Wow!" Shad strained to look out the girls' window. "The police have taped off the front door! It must be something serious!"

Serious? Katie's mind raced. "Could it be a robbery?"

Tim's face turned white under all the freckles. He sat up straight. "I sure hope Ellison Simms already banked all the money from the Harvest Dinner!"

"All right, kids—quiet down!" Judd Jones bellowed. "I don't know what's goin' on over at that church, but I'd say

Stormy Fall

the police don't need any help from you." He laughed a phlegmy laugh as the bus chugged past First Church.

But the kids on the bus couldn't keep quiet.

"See that?" called a voice from the back. "They're wheeling someone out on a stretcher!"

"What?" Katie jumped to her feet. She was quickly pitched back by the lurching school bus.

"You'd better stay down, Katie," whispered Alisha, "or Judd'll toss you off the bus."

"But those kids said 'stretcher'! Alisha, this may be even worse than a robbery at the church."

"I know." Alisha gave a little shiver as she stashed her notebook in her backpack. "It's going to be really hard to concentrate on that English test this morning...."

⌇

No one at school had heard anything about the trouble at First Church. In the Life Skills kitchen, Katie tried to measure one-and-a-half cups of flour into the mixing bowl to make bran muffins.

"Whoa, Katie!" yipped her cooking partner. "That's *three* cups of flour you put in there! You added flour twice."

"Sorry." Katie handed over the spoon and measuring cup. She stood back. "I've got something else on my mind."

The rest of her morning didn't go much better. Even her favorite class, social studies, dragged.

Well, lunch hour can't help but be an improvement, she told herself as she snatched her lunch sack from the locker.

In the crowded cafeteria she searched for a friendly face.

"Hey, Katie!" Alisha waved her arms from a table over by the wall. Katie hurried to the table.

"Did you hear any . . ." they both asked at the same time, and then stopped. They looked at each other, eyebrows arched in surprise, and giggled. The two quickly grew serious again.

"I just couldn't get into my classes this morning," Alisha said. "All I could think about was the church."

"Me, too." Katie began opening her lunch. "I hope there's something good in here, because so far, today's been the pits." She peeked in the sack. Peanut butter and jelly sandwich, carrot sticks, and an apple. She sighed.

"Here, I bought us each a carton of milk." Alisha shoved the small carton across to Katie. She glanced toward the entrance. "Well, your day is gonna be even 'better' soon, Katie. Here comes Gwen."

"Hi, Katie," Gwen said with a sunny smile, ignoring Alisha as usual. Without being invited, she plopped her lunch tray on the table and sat down. She leaned over toward Katie. "I heard there were police cars at our church this morning. Do you know anything about it, Katie?"

"Not a thing," Katie answered quickly. She bit off a big bite of gooey sandwich.

"Really? I heard it was a robbery. Aunt Berniece says we've got to do something about all these foreigners and other penniless people moving into town." She eyed Alisha. "They're ruining Mapleton."

"You're new in town, too, Gwen," said Alisha.

"Oh, that's entirely different," Gwen said scornfully. She looked at Katie's sandwich. "Peanut butter and jelly again, Katie?" She gave a little shudder. "I couldn't bear to eat a cold sandwich every day." She dipped her fork into a steaming square of lasagna.

"I happen to love peanut butter and jelly." To prove it, Katie took another giant bite of sandwich.

"Of course you do." Gwen smiled. She looked over at Alisha's cheese sandwich. "You know, girls, there's a school lunch program, so needy kids can have free hot lunches."

"Just eat your lasagna, Gwen," Katie said.

But Gwen was gazing across the crowded lunchroom. "Look, there's Tim and Shad and some of the basketball guys eating over there. I think I'll go ask them about the church. I'm so worried."

"Here, Gwen," Katie said, shoving the lunch tray toward her. "Don't forget this."

"Oh, that's all right." Gwen waved her hand back at them. "You girls can have it."

They watched her push her way through the mass of lunch eaters and squeeze onto a bench where the boys were sitting.

"Would you look at that!" Katie angrily tossed her bread crust on the table. "Tim Reilly's giving her one of his sandwiches."

"Yeah, and she's gobbling it down," said Alisha.

"And Tim always brings peanut butter and jelly!"

"Gwen will do anything to get a guy's attention." Alisha slurped her milk through a straw. "Katie, sometimes I wonder how you ever got to be friends with her."

Katie violently bit down on a carrot stick. "Gwen and I are not exactly friends, no matter what she says. She's just grabbed on to me, and she won't let go no matter how hard I try to shake her. But, you know, no matter how much she pretends, she really doesn't have an easy life." Katie poked another carrot stick into her mouth and chewed for a minute. "Sometimes, like today, I get so mad at Gwen I'd like to pinch her. Other times, though . . ."—she sighed—"all I want to do is pray for her."

"The way she's acting up for those guys, I'd like to pinch her myself," Alisha said. "Come on, Katie, grab your apple and let's take a walk outside. It may be foggy, but at least we can cool off."

The fog blanketed the whole town of Mapleton that afternoon. The kids who had hoped to see what was going on at First Church were disappointed. They could barely make out the outline of the church building through the fog curtain. Only the fluorescent yellow tape showed clearly.

Katie took the empty seat beside Tim Reilly on the bus. Alisha's mom had picked her up for a dental appointment.

"So, where's Shad?" Katie asked Tim. "I thought you two were like Siamese twins."

"He's trying out for basketball. The team'll be practicing almost every afternoon from now on."

"How come you didn't try out, Tim? You're pretty good when the kids play at church."

Tim sighed and stretched his lanky arms. "Yeah, I'd like to, but I've got my afternoon paper route. I wanna help out my mom—take off some of the pressure of raising six kids."

Katie nodded. "I'm glad Mom only has to work three nights a week." She looked outside at the grayness. "I was thinking of trying out for girls' volleyball, but now I guess I'm going to be on the cheerleading squad instead."

"You're going to be one of the cheerleaders? Congratulations, Katie. When did you find out?"

Stormy Fall

"Well, it isn't absolutely official yet, but Sue Wong practically told me at the Harvest Dinner. She's the head cheerleader."

"Yeah, I like Sue." Tim grinned. "But I bet you'd pack a real wallop serving a volleyball, Katie."

"I do pack a wallop." Katie grinned and flexed her arm muscle. "Just ask my little brother, Alex. It'll be a real honor to be a cheerleader, though."

"Yeah, I guess so." Tim stared out the bus window. "Man, I wish we could see the church. I guess we'll have to wait 'til we get home to find out what happened."

"Well, it won't be long now." Katie cringed as the bus rattled over the railroad tracks. She watched the dim outlines of the store buildings as they passed through town. One of the newer, classier shops was Ellison Simms's flower shop. Phoebe Phillips's younger cousin had been away when Katie's family had stayed in Phoebe's apartment. Katie was glad of that. She agreed with Nurse Fish; Ellison Simms was a snob. Katie waved at Tim when he got off at his stop. Now he'd have to get his bike and collect the papers for his afternoon paper route.

The air brakes hissed at her stop and the door swung open. Katie was ready, and dashed down the steps. Judd didn't like anyone dillydallying around. "See ya," she called to the few kids left on the bus.

Today the fall leaves didn't crackle under her feet—they were soggy clumps because of the rain. Katie ran up the wooden steps. She stooped to pet Little Mike on the head as she wiped her feet on the mat.

"I'm home, Mom!" she called as she opened the door. She heard squeals and shrieks and thumping upstairs. Hannah must have her neighborhood friends visiting again.

Mom came into the living room, wiping her hands on a towel. "I'm working in the kitchen. Come on in, Katie."

Katie shrugged off her heavy backpack and windbreaker. "That fog is thick this afternoon, but I guess that's nothing new." She crammed her jacket in the tiny hall closet and walked out to the kitchen.

Mom looked up and smiled. "Folks have warned me that when the fall rains start, we'll wish the fog was still here." She was up to her elbows in sticky, squishy dough.

"Are you making bread?" asked Katie. "How come?"

Her mom dumped the mass of dough onto a floured breadboard. "I just had a longing for some of your grandma's homemade wheat bread. I guess I'm a bit homesick."

"Me, too." Katie sat down at the kitchen table. "Sometimes my stomach hurts, I get so lonesome for everyone back in Sunnydale." She looked at a bowl of apples and picked up the biggest and reddest one. "Hey, Mom, I think something bad happened at the church last night. When the bus drove by there this morning, we saw a lot of lights and police cars. Some of the kids said they saw medics taking out someone on a stretcher."

"I know." Mom began pounding and kneading the ball of dough. "Mrs. Reilly said the poor soul was unconscious and nearly dead when Pastor Miller got to the church this morning."

"Do they know who it is?"

"Yes, as a matter of fact." Mom lifted her sticky hands from the mound of dough. "It was Stella Tootle."

The apple fell from Katie's hand. "Stella? Mom, is she going to be all right?"

Stormy Fall

Her mom wiped her hands on the towel again and walked over to put her hands on Katie's shoulder. "We don't know, dear. She has a fractured skull, and she's still unconscious."

Katie put her face in her hands. "How did it happen?"

"She must have fallen down the stairs by Pastor Miller's office sometime Sunday night. The police don't know yet whether someone hit her on the head or whether she hit it on the stair banister. It looks pretty bad, Katie."

Suddenly Katie raised her head. "Edith? How's Edith? Is she all right?"

Mom walked back over to her bread dough. "Good question." She pounded the elastic dough with her fist, turned it over, and began pounding the other side. "Our friend Edith seems to have disappeared. Edith and all the money collected from the Harvest Dinner and the Sunday church services."

Chapter Seven

Katie stooped to pick up the apple she had dropped. She squeezed it tightly between her hands. "Mom, do you think Edith was kidnapped or is maybe even... dead?"

Her mom had now sliced the big mound of dough into four pieces. "I just don't know, Katie." She shaped each of the four pieces into a loaf and put them into bread pans to rise. "All we can do is pray that police find her in time." Mom looked up toward the noise upstairs. "Katie, why don't you go tell the little Reilly girls it's nearly four. Mrs. Reilly wanted them home by then."

"Good!" said Katie. "From the noise those kids have been making up there, I wouldn't be surprised to see our bedroom drop down through the ceiling."

She soon had Tim's two little red-haired sisters, Megan and Sally, into their coats and out the front door. She and Hannah walked them to the gate and watched them go all the way down the street to the small green house where they lived.

As they waited by the gate, a large blue sedan pulled into the driveway and stopped. Alex hopped out. "See ya tomorrow, Skip." The car pulled away, and Alex knelt to give Little Mike a hug.

Stormy Fall

"So, you've been up to your new friend's house again?" Katie said.

"Yep." Alex gave Little Mike a pat and started up the steps.

"You stayed overnight with him Sunday night and you were over there again today? I guess you really like Skip, huh?"

Alex shrugged. "Skip's cool." He turned and went into the house.

Katie watched him close the door. *Alex and I did everything together this summer,* she thought. *Now we don't even talk to each other.* She shivered and then snatched up Hannah's little hand. "Let's go in the house, Hannah. It's cold out here."

Late Tuesday afternoon, Tim rode up to their house to leave a newspaper. "I had a couple of extra newspapers from my route. Thought maybe your family would like to read one—especially since First Church made the front page."

"Thanks, Tim." Katie took the paper, unfolded it, and gasped. There in full color was a big picture of their church building circled by police cars and bright lights. A second picture showed poor Stella's crumpled figure, lying at the foot of the office stairway.

". . . unconscious transient woman . . . large amount of missing money . . . second transient suspect missing . . ."

Katie stopped reading. "Oh, Tim, this is horrible. You don't think the police suspect Edith of being the thief, do you?"

"No way!" he scoffed. "I sure hope the police find her soon, though. So we'll know she's okay." He turned his bike and pedaled out to the road. "By the way, our youth group will be meeting at Good Sam House tomorrow night. I guess the church building is still taped off as the scene of a crime."

"Well, maybe everything'll be better by tomorrow evening," Katie said hopefully.

"Maybe." Tim didn't sound optimistic as he crossed the street and pedaled home.

⁓

Nothing had changed by Wednesday evening. The police had reported no progress. Stella still lay in the hospital in a coma. Edith and the money remained missing.

A small group of quiet kids met on the porch of the big house. When they went inside, their feet clunked loudly as they walked through the empty rooms. The Kippers were waiting for them in the bare living room.

Short, happy Ed Kipper wasn't happy tonight. "There's no use pretending things are normal this evening, guys. We had a terrible tragedy hit our church Sunday night." He stood there with his hands jammed in his pockets and his head hanging. "A member of our church—a good woman—is lying unconscious at this very moment. Another one is still missing."

"Along with nearly four thousand dollars," someone muttered.

Ed nodded. "Yes, there is the money, too. But of course, the human lives are more important." Finally, his face crinkled into his normal happy smile. "But we're not going to let this get us down, are we, guys?"

"No," came the weak reply.

"We're going to put all this in the hands of the Lord, right?"

"Right!" The answer was louder this time.

Ed's grin spread even wider. "Is God all powerful?" he shouted.

Stormy Fall

"Yes!" the kids shouted back.

"Okay! Now, when the church fixes Good Sam House into a shelter, our group will be in charge of painting one room—including picking the color, if we don't get too wild. Any suggestions?"

Katie waved her hand. "Daffodil yellow. Daffodils are one of Edith's favorite flowers."

"Daffodil yellow? What do the rest of you think?"

"Daffodil yellow!" echoed the kids' voices.

"Man, we're starting to sound like a cheer squad," said Tim.

Claudia Curtiss and Gwen Van Switt, who had just walked into the house, stopped and stared. "What's going on?" Claudia said.

Ed laughed. "The rest of the guys just picked the new color for one of the bedrooms in Good Sam House."

Claudia looked at Gwen and raised her plucked eyebrows. "Do you guys really think the church is going to go ahead with plans to put this homeless shelter right next door after what happened Sunday night?" Claudia said.

"Oh, come on, Claudia!" said Katie. "It's already been okayed by the church board *and* the trustees!"

Claudia slowly shook her head from side to side. Her frizzy red-blond hair swished across her face. "My mother says they're planning another vote to cancel that."

"But poor Edith and Stella will need a place to live more than ever now!" Alisha argued.

"Sorry, guys," said Gwen in a sad voice. "From what we hear from very good sources, Edith and Stella are the reason there will *never* be a Good Sam House."

"What?" roared Katie.

Stormy Fall

"Think about it, guys," Claudia said. "Those two penniless old bag ladies sneaked into the church Sunday night. Because they were church janitors, it was easy for them to learn the safe combination. They unlocked the safe and stole all the money from Saturday night's dinner and the Sunday offering."

Gwen put her arm around Katie's shoulder. "Then Edith decided she wanted it all, so she shoved her sister down the stairs and escaped with everything. I'm so sorry, Katie, but it all fits."

Katie shoved Gwen's hand away. "None of it fits! If you two snobs had ever taken the time to get to know the Tootle sisters, you'd understand they could never do anything like that. Besides, Edith loved her sister more than anyone else in the world...." She stopped. "Oh, what's the use."

"Now, now," soothed Gwen. "I don't want to think that my dear friend Katie Barnes is having a pity party."

Katie clenched her fists. "I am not having a pity party! And for the last time, Gwen, *we*..."

Gwen ignored her. "I'm glad of that, Katie." She glanced across the room. "Oh, there's Tim! I want to talk to him. I'm having a problem with my math, and he's so helpful. Tim! Hey, Tim!" She waved her hand. "I'll see you girls later. *Ciao!*"

As she walked away, Alisha sneered. "Since when did Gwen start worrying about homework?"

Katie glared as she watched the bubbly blond flounce away. "Since she saw Tim over there. It makes me so mad the way she chases him!"

Alisha looked at Katie and grinned.

By the time the youth meeting ended, the misty fog had

lifted and a pale moon showed through. Except for the yellow tape across the front, the church building looked the same as it had a week ago.

"Everything's so peaceful now. It's hard to believe all those terrible things happened just last Sunday night," said Joan Kipper softly as they all walked over to the parking lot.

"Yes, and Saturday night had been so wonderful," agreed her husband.

"And didn't everyone at the dinner just love Edith and Stella?" Alisha asked. "I thought people would never quit clapping after they sang."

Shad had hurried ahead of the rest of them to shoot a couple of baskets at the church hoop. Now he jogged back. "And it was one big surprise to hear Stella sing. None of us had ever heard her say a single word before that!"

"Yeah, and she belted out 'Bringing in the Sheaves' like a pro," Katie said. She snatched the basketball from Shad and dribbled over to the hoop. Katie made a shot, and the ball thumped against the backboard before swishing through the net. Tim tried to grab the ball, but Katie ducked in, grabbed it again, and made another perfect basket.

"Hey, nice shots, Katie!" Sue said as she walked past.

"Thanks, Sue," Katie said. Then, sighing, she turned back to her friends. "Mom had invited the Tootles over for Thanksgiving at our place this year."

"Well, maybe they can still come," said Alisha. "Cheer up, Katie. Thanksgiving's still almost three weeks off."

Mr. Emery studied the glum faces that were getting into his van. "We're going by Smitty's Ice Cream Parlor for double-scoop ice cream cones," he announced. "Buckle up, everyone!"

Stormy Fall

Katie was delivered to her front door at ten that night. "Tell your dad it's my fault you're late, Katie," Mr. Emery said with a chuckle. "You can't hurry with Smitty's double-scoop cones. Then tell him I'll pick him up to go steelhead fishing on the river the first Saturday I get off from work."

"I'll tell him," Katie promised.

When Katie delivered the message, her dad's chuckle was almost as deep as Mr. Emery's had been. "Now *that*, Katie, is the best part of moving to a new place. We make great new friends like the Emerys." Dad yawned and stretched. "Guess I'll be off to bed, now that you're home safe." He pulled off his reading glasses and pointed with them at the folded newspaper Tim had dropped off the day before. "That's a terrible thing that happened at the church Sunday night. I was looking at those pictures in the paper." He shook his head. "We've got to trust the Lord to bring Edith and Stella safely through this."

He gave Katie a hug. "The Tootles are two of the best friends we've made here in Mapleton, Katie Lou. Folks who think they could be to blame for this robbery, why, they just don't know them like we do."

"Thanks, Dad," Katie said. She watched him walk toward her parents' bedroom. *He's getting stoop-shouldered, working so hard,* Katie thought sadly.

The steep staircase squeaked with each step as Katie climbed toward the upstairs bedrooms. She peeked into Alex's dark room. *Thump, thump, thump* pounded Little Mike's tail on the floor. Katie just grinned as she quietly closed the door.

Chapter Eight

*I*t was a dark gray morning.

Hannah sat at the kitchen table, her elbow on the table top. She plopped her spoon up and down in the soggy bowl of cornflakes. "Can't we have cream of wheat with raisins, Katie?" she whined. "That's what Mommy fixes me."

"Eat your cornflakes," snapped Katie. She was standing at the counter dipping her knife into a large jar of peanut butter. She slopped it onto three slices of bread.

Alex came thundering down the stairs. He looked around the kitchen. "Where's Mom?"

"She's in bed with a headache." Katie spread margarine on three more slices of bread.

"Well, where's my clean blue jeans? Mom promised she'd wash them yesterday. They're not in the drawer."

Katie slammed the sticky knife on the counter. She silently counted to ten.

"Go check in the dryer, Alex. Maybe Mom washed them and didn't get them folded." She watched him stomp out to the glassed-in back porch. Katie heard the dryer door open.

"Yeah, they're in here, Katie, but they're all wrinkled. Can you press 'em for me?"

Stormy Fall

Katie had just picked up the jam jar. She set it down gently. "Alex, this is a great chance for you to learn how to iron your own clothes. As you can see, I'm busy fixing our lunches." She slapped the slices of bread together and crammed the sandwiches into plastic bags.

"I guess these jeans aren't too wrinkled," Alex said. He went back upstairs carrying the unironed jeans.

Katie looked back at her little sister. "You'd better go up and wash your hands and face and get dressed, Hannah." Hannah whimpered all the way upstairs.

Alone in the kitchen, Katie glanced up at the clock as she started to peel carrots. Great! She wasn't even going to have time to eat breakfast herself.

Katie looked up as her mom walked into the kitchen, her face pale. "Thanks, Katie. I needed that extra hour."

"Mom, those two kids are the pits in the morning," Katie said as she rolled down the tops of the lunch sacks. "Sometimes I don't know how you and Dad put up with us."

"A little patience and a lot of love, Katie," replied Mom with a tired smile. "Now you'd better get your things ready to go. The bus is almost here."

Katie barely had time to grab her own lunch sack as the angry beep-beep of Jed Judd's school bus sped her out the front door.

"Slept in again, huh?" Jed scowled as she dashed into the bus with only one arm in the sleeve of her windbreaker. "You know buses have a schedule to keep, don't you?"

Katie opened her mouth, then closed it again. She stood without speaking until she could unclench her teeth. "Thanks for waiting, Mr. Judd." A little patience and a lot of love, huh?

Jed only grunted as he slammed the door shut and released the air brakes.

"Over here, Katie!" called Alisha, motioning to the empty seat beside her.

Katie sat down with a groan. "I'm so glad you saved me a seat. It's the best thing that's happened this morning. Have you heard any more news about Edith and Stella?"

"Nothing good. My dad said he heard they haven't been staying at the motel for the past week or two. Police think they've been sleeping in that old shed behind the church."

"You're kidding! Well, they probably couldn't afford the motel. Some social service group paid their rent for a few weeks."

Alisha nodded. "But if they'd only let Pastor Miller know they couldn't afford the rent, I'm sure the church would have helped them."

Katie slipped off her backpack and stashed it on the floor. "The Tootles may not have much money, but they still have their pride."

"Yeah, but that's not the worst of the news."

"So give me the rest of it," Katie said with a sigh.

"Well, the police also think the Tootles have been sleeping nights in the church basement since it's gotten colder."

"Now, how could they get inside at night? They don't have their own key. They've had to do all the janitoring during the day because some of the church members, like Phoebe, don't trust them with a key."

"It's simple," replied Alisha. "The police found a little wedge of wood stuck in the crack of the basement door. That way, the door lock couldn't catch. There were some old coats in a pile in the furnace room, too. It looked like they'd been sleeping there." Alisha looked over at Katie. "Edith's wallet was lying under the coats, Katie. Sorry I couldn't give you any better news."

Katie just sat there with her eyes shut. "Wait!" Her eyes popped open as she turned to face Alisha. "You did give me some good news! Thank you!"

"I did?"

"You said the police found Edith's wallet, right?"

Alisha looked blank but nodded.

"So Edith and Stella were asleep Sunday night in the furnace room. Then they must have heard someone prowling around upstairs. And they went up to check it out. Do you understand now, Alisha?"

"Nope."

"Look, if the sisters had planned to sneak upstairs, steal the offerings, and run away, Edith would have taken her wallet. I'm sure of it. People keep their pictures and important stuff like that in their wallets. Especially homeless people. Edith was sharp, Alisha. She wouldn't have left that wallet unless she was planning to come right back. Anyway, how could they have opened the safe?"

Alisha's brow wrinkled. "If the Tootles didn't steal that money, more'n likely it was someone in the church who knew what was in the safe only until Monday morning. Who's gonna believe that person did it when they can blame two penniless, homeless old women?"

"Me, for one," Katie replied, just as their bus pulled into line behind a long string of yellow buses near the school entrance.

Stormy Fall

"Guess we're here." Alisha stood up and got in line to get off the bus. "See you at lunchtime. Whoever gets to the cafeteria first saves seats."

"Right." Katie shifted her sliding backpack. "We've got to do something about this mystery. We can plan our MO while we eat lunch."

"Our what?"

"Our modus operandi—you know, our plan of action." Katie swung off the bus behind her friend.

But Katie didn't have a chance to work out an MO with Alisha during their lunch break. She had barely sat down at the cafeteria table across from Alisha and Janie Dawson when Gwen dashed up to them.

"Oh, Katie," she said, "I've been looking for you all morning. I thought I should tell you first. But I suppose it's too late now."

"What's too late?" asked Katie.

"Well, have you been down to the gym to see the bulletin board?"

Katie began to open her lunch sack. "No, I don't have PE on Friday. Why, what's on it that's so important?"

"It's the list. You know, listing the names of the two new cheerleaders."

Katie's hand froze on her lunch sack. "Who's on the list?"

"That's what I wanted to tell you. It's . . . uh, Claudia and me, Katie."

Katie's tongue felt thick when she tried to speak. "And—and not me?"

Gwen gently shook her head without mussing a single blond hair. "I wanted to tell you the bad news myself. But don't feel

Stormy Fall

bad, Katie. Lots of other girls weren't good enough, either." She gave Katie a pat on the shoulder. "I've got to run now. We're having a short cheerleaders meeting right after lunch today."

"Oh, Katie, that's a bummer," said Alisha after Gwen had breezed away.

"I saw the list this morning on my way to PE," said Janie. "Honestly, you should have seen Gwen. She jumped up and down like a five-year-old when she saw her name."

Katie sat and looked down at her lunch sack so the girls couldn't see the tears in her eyes.

"It's just not fair!" Alisha said as she stared across the room at Gwen. "I'm sure you were much better than her."

"If it'll make you feel any better, Katie," said Janie, "I heard one of the other cheerleaders say that if Sue Wong hadn't voted against you, you would have made it."

Katie's head jerked up. "Sue voted against me? But Sue's my friend! Sue told me I was terrific at the tryouts."

Janie shook her head. "Sorry, Katie, I'm just telling you what I heard."

"It's okay." Katie took her sandwich from the sack and unwrapped it. She peeled back a corner of the top slice of bread. "Oh, no! Just peanut butter!" She angrily shoved the sandwich back into her lunch sack. "Wouldn't you know? I forgot to put on jam when I made my sandwich this morning!" She felt tears roll down her cheeks.

"Oh, Katie, don't cry about your sandwich," begged Alisha.

Janie held a plastic-wrapped package over to her. "Here, let's trade sandwiches, Katie. Mine is tuna fish again. I love peanut butter. Mom won't let us have it in the house because my little sister's allergic to peanuts."

And all at once, for no apparent reason, Katie felt the corners of her mouth trying to turn up. No matter how hard she tried to stop it, she felt a giggle bubbling in her throat. And the giggle turned into a laugh.

Alisha and Janie stared at her. Alisha began to shake her arm. "Katie, are you okay?"

Katie could only bob her head up and down. "I'm fine," she finally gasped. "I was just thinking how crazy I must have looked—crying because I have a peanut butter sandwich."

Now her two friends joined her in laughing. "We've got to stop this," Janie said. "Everyone's staring at us."

"You're right." Katie wiped tears of laughter from her eyes. "I was really boo-hooing like a baby because I didn't get picked for cheerleader. Pretty dumb, huh?" She took her peanut butter sandwich from the sack again and handed it to Janie. Then she unwrapped the tuna sandwich and took a big bite. "Umm, good."

"Mine, too," Janie mumbled around a mouthful of sticky peanut butter. "Homemade bread, too! This is great."

"My mom made it," Katie said. "Mom's a terrific cook." She looked from one girl to the other. "Maybe today's been good for me. I know I learned a couple of things, anyway."

"Like what?" Alisha slurped her carton of milk.

Katie reached out a hand to both of them. "Like I learned who my friends are." Her smile faded. "I learned another thing, too; I learned there's a really thick wall of fog between us in Lower Mapleton and the ones who live up on the hill. And they're gonna try to keep us from getting through that wall. They may pretend they care about us or like us, but they don't."

"Oh, Katie, that's not right," Alisha said. "I know Sue Wong likes you. She likes all of us. She's a good Christian."

Katie shrugged. "So? She still lives in a swanky house on the hill. Her mom and dad are both attorneys. So, she picks a klutz like Gwen over me just because Gwen lives up there and buys her clothes at fancy boutiques." Katie wadded her empty lunch sack and stood up. "Now, I've got to go to the library."

By the time she got home from school Friday afternoon Katie had convinced herself that losing out as a cheerleader was the best thing that could have happened to her. *Grandma Ross would say I was getting too big for my britches,* she thought. *Here I was thinking I could do anything those kids up on the hill could do. I even thought some of them, like Sue, were going to be my friends. Ha!* She kicked at a pile of leaves. *At least now I know where I stand. It's going to be "us" against "them."* Katie clenched her fist. *And we're gonna win!*

As the school bus pulled away in a dark cloud of exhaust smoke, Katie pushed open the rickety front gate to her yard.

Bam! Bam! Someone was hammering in the backyard. She cut across to the back and saw Alex working on the doghouse.

He looked up and saw her. "Mom discovered Little Mike in my bedroom this morning." He grinned. "You were right, Katie. She says he has to sleep out here, so I'm fixing the roof on his house to keep the rain out."

"Good," Katie said. "That big dog really stinks up your bedroom." She sat on the back porch step and watched.

"Little Mike doesn't stink. Do you, boy?" Alex tossed the hammer onto the dead grass and ran over to grab his dog in a headlock. The two started rolling around on the dead grass,

Little Mike's tongue lolling out the side of his big mouth. Katie had to laugh at the two of them.

She stood and walked closer. "Something fell out of your pocket, Alex." She bent down and picked up a ten dollar bill. "Wait a minute! This is money! Alex, where did you get a ten dollar bill?" She stared at his hip pocket. "Hey! You've got even more in your pocket! What's going on here, Alex? Where did you get those bills?"

Chapter Nine

Alex leaped up, his wet curls plastered against his round, sweaty face. "You give that back, Katie!" He snatched the ten dollar bill and ran up the porch steps. "This money's mine!"

"Then tell me where you got it—and the other bills I saw in your pocket." Katie started up the steps after him.

"No way! It's none of your business!" Alex clamped his hand over his hip pocket. "Don't go blabbing to Mom and Dad about this, either. I wanna surprise 'em with a—a cool present for their wedding anniversary. You probably didn't even remember that their anniversary's almost here."

Katie stopped on the step. Alex was right. She had forgotten all about her folks' anniversary. It must be next week.

Quickly, Alex stuffed the bill back in his pocket, dashed into the kitchen, and slammed the door hard.

Katie laid her hand on Little Mike's shaggy head. "Oh, Little Mike," she said softly. "What kind of trouble is Alex in now?" The dog huddled close to her, his tail tucked between his legs.

Katie slumped down on the step. If something was wrong, it was probably because of that new friend of his, Skip. Alex had gone up on the hill a few times to visit Skip, and now he had money falling out of his pockets. Until now, Alex hadn't had a spare quarter all fall.

Stormy Fall

She should warn her brother about making friends with those kids up on the hill. Katie thought of Sue. Even when she'd pretended to be Katie's friend, she'd shown her true colors soon enough.

Oh, well, like Grandma Ross always said, "Worrying never solved anything." This was the weekend, and Katie planned to enjoy herself. Besides, Alex probably wouldn't listen to her advice anyway. It seemed like the last thing he wanted was for his big sister to tell him what to do. She gave Little Mike a last scratch between his floppy ears, then stood.

Saturday morning did not get off to a great start. Katie woke with a jolt to the ripping, tearing sound of walls being taken apart. She sat up in bed, fully awake. What was going on in Alex's room? She jumped out of bed and pulled on her old terry-cloth robe and slippers.

When she opened her brother's door, a cloud of plaster dust smacked her in the face. Dad was up on a stepladder, prying wallboard from the walls.

"Dad, what are you doing in here?"

"Huh? Oh, sorry, Katie, did I wake you up?" Dad climbed down and looked proudly at the destroyed wall. "Well, since your brother's going to stay overnight with his friend again, I thought I'd do a little repair work. This old wallboard is moldy and crumbling, and I'm going to replace it."

Katie sighed. "I guess I didn't need to sleep in anyway." She pushed a dusty cover from a corner of Alex's bed and sat down. "Dad, do you and Mom think it's a good idea for Alex to spend so much time at Skip Young's house? What if he's a bad influence on Alex? I mean, what do we really know about Skip's family other than they live in a big house up on the hill?"

Stormy Fall

"What do we know about them? Well, let's see...." Dad perched on one of the steps of the ladder. "We know they're a Christian family. We know they're in the Lord's house every Sunday. We know that Skip's mom died when he was only two. His dad's raising him and his brother alone and doing a pretty good job, too. Right now the boys are studying about Native Americans, and Skip and Alex are working on a model village with teepees and all."

"Okay, okay, I was just wondering. I hope Skip's as perfect as he sounds." She stood up and brushed plaster scraps from her robe, sneezing from the thick dust. "I guess I'd better go downstairs and see what the rest of the family are up to."

When she walked into the kitchen, she saw Alex and Hannah at the table, eating pancakes. Mom was sitting at the far end of the table with a pen in her hand and her checkbook and a stack of bills in front of her.

"Good morning, everyone," Katie said.

Mom looked up. "Good morning, sleepyhead. I'm glad you finally came downstairs."

"Yeah, maybe you can take your own phone calls for a change," mumbled Alex around a mouthful of pancakes.

"I've had phone calls?"

"Three of them," said Mom. "From Tim. I promised him you'd call as soon as you got up."

Katie glanced over at the wall clock. "Ten o'clock? I can't believe it. Guess it's a good thing Dad's project woke me up." Walking over to the phone, she dialed Tim.

"Hey, Katie!" Tim's enthusiastic voice shouted in her ear. "What do you think about the weather today?"

"What?" Katie turned and stared out the window for the

first time that morning. "It's sunny!" She turned to her family. "Look outside, everyone! The sun's shining! The dreary old fog's gone. And there's no rain."

"Not 'gone,' necessarily," Tim said. "It'll probably be back tomorrow. The guys decided we should do something fun today. How about you, Katie?"

"Sure. What've you got in mind?"

"The plan was to hike down to the Green River and watch the coho salmon run. Shad's dad was out there fishing yesterday. He says the salmon are running so thick in places, a guy could walk right across the river on their backs. Not that we'd want to do that," he added quickly.

After checking with her mom, Katie agreed that the hike sounded like a great idea.

"Oh, and Alisha said to tell you to be sure and wear old clothes," Tim said. "It might be a little rough down along the riverbank."

Katie laughed. "Like I have any other kind of clothes," she said as she hung up.

"Well, you better eat your breakfast if you're going on a hike, Katie," Mom said. "And maybe you can wear a heavy sweatshirt under that flimsy jacket. It's still cold outside. And be careful not to get too near the water."

"Yes, Mom," Katie said with a grin. "We'll be fine."

Katie was waiting out by the roadside by one that afternoon. Besides her sweatshirt and jacket, she wore Alex's red knit stocking cap pulled low over her ears. She felt like a little four-year-old crammed into a winter snowsuit.

She was glad to see that the kids hiking down the road toward her didn't look much better. That was one of the good things about living in Lower Mapleton. No one bought their clothes in those fancy clothing stores.

"The river road is about a half mile further down this street, Katie," Shad said. "We'll follow it until we find a good place to get down to the riverbank."

"Sounds good," Katie said. She fell into step beside Janie and Alisha.

"There's only one rule on this hike," said Tim. He was wearing blue-and-green plaid earmuffs over his ears.

"We're not gonna talk about any problems going on at church or at school today. We're just gonna enjoy the sunshine and being outdoors."

"Right!" agreed Katie.

The hike wasn't exactly like an outing back home. Traffic whizzed back and forth on the road. They had to walk by a new development of houses as well as an apartment building. Still, they all agreed it was a terrific way to spend Saturday afternoon.

When the road forked off to follow the river, there was less traffic and fewer houses. The alder and maple trees were mostly bare black branches in November, but the evergreen trees were still green and perky.

Alisha stopped. "Oh, listen to the bird chirping!"

Shad cocked his head. "Sounds like a chickadee. Or it could be a junco."

"Well, I know what that blue one over there is." Katie pointed up into a bare maple tree. "It's a blue jay. We saw a lot of them this summer while we were living in a campground."

Tim had walked ahead and now he beckoned the others

Stormy Fall

to follow him. "This is a good trail down to the river. See? There's a lot of bank where we can walk."

"Oh, it's gorgeous," said Katie. When they reached the river, she looked across the swift-running water to the green foliage and trees on the other side. "I'm so glad we came out here this afternoon."

"Let's walk down this way, and we should find a good place to see the salmon," Shad said. They all walked single-file behind him. When anyone spoke, it was in a hushed voice.

"This almost feels like we're in church, doesn't it?" Tim said.

"Shhh! Look!" Shad pointed out across the sparkling blue-green running water. There, swimming against the current, were dozens—maybe hundreds—of the silvery salmon. Their backs and top fins showed above the water. No one spoke. They just drank in the sight with their eyes.

After about fifteen minutes they turned and slowly retraced their steps.

"Hold it, guys! Look over there!" Janie pointed to a tiny treeless island in the middle of the river. A blue heron stood as motionless as a statue on its tall, spindly legs. As they watched, the bird's head suddenly darted into the water and came back out with a small salmon—or perhaps it was a trout—in its beak. The heron swallowed the wriggling fish and took off down the river, its great wings spread wide.

"Awesome!" breathed Alisha.

"Well, guys, I guess we'd better be getting back to the road," said Shad. "Some hike, huh?"

As they all slowly turned and followed Shad and Tim, Mark Gomez stooped and picked up a crumpled beer can. He held it out. "Now, this is the kind of thing that ticks me off! God

Stormy Fall

gives us this beautiful world and what do people do? They clutter it all up with their garbage!" He reached into his backpack and pulled out a couple of folded plastic bags. "Come on, guys, let's collect some of this junk as we walk along. I try to do it whenever I'm out like this." He dropped the beer can into one bag and handed the other bag to Tim.

No one said much as they began to notice and pick up bottles, cans, paper cartons, and other clutter along the river edge. Tim stepped over to a small group of cattails and bent down. "Look, I found an old Mariners baseball cap!" The late afternoon sun glinted on the cap as Tim held it high. He opened the top of the plastic bag.

"Wait a minute, Tim!" shouted Katie. She stumbled and nearly fell over a fallen log as she hurried over to him. "Let me see that cap!"

"It's pretty gross, Katie," warned Tim.

"I don't care. I just want to see it." She snatched the soggy cap by the bill and brushed mud from the front of it. "Look!" As she held the cap out to the others, the sun glinted on a tiny gold cross pinned to the cap.

"This is Edith Tootle's cap," she said. "It has to be!"

"I don't know, Katie," Shad said. "It could belong to half the people in King County."

"With a gold cross pinned on the front? I don't think so." Katie was not going to be talked down on this. "Somehow, Edith's cap, which she always wears, has made it down here to the bank of the Green River. So, where's Edith?"

Janie had been poking around the cattails with a stick. Now, she lifted up what looked like a small plastic bag. "Here's something else." The kids quickly gathered around her.

Stormy Fall

"Wait, I've got gloves." Mark pulled a pair of thin rubber gloves from his backpack and slipped them on. He took the bag and carefully untwisted the wire that closed it. Putting his hand into the sodden bag, he drew out three pieces of paper that looked like checks. The checks had patches of mold on them, but most of the writing was still readable. "Harvest Dinner," read Mark out loud. He studied the other check. "Harvest Dinner." He looked up. "One of them is for $25 and one of them is for $40."

"Put the checks back in the bag, Mark," Tim said. He looked over at Katie. "You guys wait right here; I'll go to the nearest house and call 9-1-1."

They all stood there and watched Tim's lanky figure as he wove his way up the steep trail to the road beyond. As if the first act of a play had ended, the sun seemed to fade away in the sky and the thick fog curtain came down.

Alisha shivered. "It's starting to get cold," she complained. "Why do we have to stay down here? Why can't we go home?"

"Because we're going to have to show the police just where we found this stuff," replied Shad. "They may have to drag the river out there."

Katie looked out over the swift-running Green River. "Why would they drag the river?"

"For Edith's body."

"No! That's stupid! Sure, I'll vouch that that old cap belonged to Edith Tootle. But that doesn't prove Edith drowned in the river. I figure these are just clues left behind by the thief."

"Then where is Edith?" asked Mark. "The police haven't located a sign of her since the theft. They're going to be real glad to get this Mariners cap—and the checks, too."

Stormy Fall

Shad sat down on a big moss-covered rock. "I'll tell you one thing, guys. Whoever broke into our church and stole the offering stole a lot more than a few thousand dollars. From what I've been hearing, they stole Good Samaritan House, too! Dad doesn't think the project has a chance now."

"And after they know we found Edith's cap and some of the missing checks, the whole town will think she's guilty," Alisha said.

A sober-faced group of kids met Tim when he rejoined them. Another fifteen minutes passed before a couple of state patrolmen in their tan uniforms joined them and began their inspection and questions.

It was five o'clock when the weary hikers trooped back into Lower Mapleton. Katie was the first one to turn in at her home.

"Oh, Katie," called Alisha. "Could you come over to my house and stay tomorrow afternoon? My folks are driving up to Everett to visit Aunt Salome, and she is *sooo* boring. They said I can stay home if you stay with me."

"Sure," Katie said. "I know it'll be fine with my folks." She made a little face. "It'll be nice to spend a peaceful afternoon after today."

Chapter Ten

*I*t started to rain again on Sunday morning.

"Oops.... Excuse me.... Sorry, ma'am." Katie elbowed her way down the front steps through the Sunday morning "after-church" crowd.

"Katie, wait!"

Katie blinked away raindrops and turned to see Alisha pushing toward her. Katie stopped. "It's okay, Alisha. I'll be ready to go with you and your folks in a second. First I have to see someone in the parking lot."

"But it's not okay, Katie. That's what I wanted to tell you. I was supposed to ask you if your parents could drop us by my place. My folks have already left for Everett."

"That won't work either! My parents just pulled out! They promised to take Hannah to McDonald's for lunch today. So what'll we do?"

Alisha looked out across the parking lot. "Hey, no problem. My uncle Jake's van is still here. I'll go catch him." She started back up the steps, then stopped. "Where will I find you, Katie?"

Katie made a face. "I'll be standing right beside Phoebe Phillips's shiny maroon Cadillac. She's not driving away until I remind her again about that money she owes me, even if I have to soak myself to the bone to do it!"

Stormy Fall

The brand-new Cadillac sedan waited in the front row of the parking lot. Everyone at church knew this was Phoebe's unofficial spot. Katie leaned against a glossy front fender and shivered. It was getting colder, and a wet, misty wind yanked at her windbreaker.

"Hey, Katie, why are you standing out here in the rain?" Tim called as he and his mom walked past her.

"I'm waiting to talk to Phoebe, but if she doesn't hurry up, I'll be too cold to say anything."

Mrs. Reilly slowed. "Katie, I'd say it's about time you started wearing a winter jacket."

"I think you're right," Katie said through chattering teeth. She watched as the ancient Reilly car filled up with Tim, his mom, and the little Reillys. They waved as they pulled out and started down the road. Where was Phoebe anyway?

"Why, Katie, it's nice to see you again." Mrs. Fish, Phoebe's nurse, walked up to the car jangling a key ring in her hand.

"Hi, Mrs. Fish. I didn't know you were still staying with Phoebe."

"Oh, I'm not. She doesn't need me. With that new cane of hers she gets around almost as well as she did before the accident. She only wanted me to drive her to church. I wish she'd hurry." Mrs. Fish smiled at Katie. "What about you? Don't tell me you're going home with her again."

"No," Katie said through stiff lips. "I just want to ask her when I'm going to get my pay for last time."

"She hasn't paid you yet?" Nurse Fish's eyes flashed behind her steel-rimmed glasses. "That woman!" She clicked her tongue and quickly unlocked the car. "I'll go see if I can speed her up and maybe give her a piece of my mind." She motioned at the empty back seat. "You climb in here and warm up, young lady. I'll be back in a jiffy."

Katie didn't argue. She jumped inside, found a plaid wool robe, and wrapped it around herself. As she reached to close the door, Alisha came speeding up. "Katie, my aunt and my cousins are already gone. One of the deacons told me Uncle Jake is in a meeting. I guess they brought two cars. We'll just have to wait until he comes out." She leaned to look inside the car. "What are you doing in Phoebe's car?"

Katie quickly explained. "Hop in. We can both snuggle under this robe while we wait. And shut the door, Alisha. I already look like a drowned rat."

"I hope it's okay with Phoebe if we sit in her car," said Alisha nervously.

"Don't worry." Katie pulled one side of the warm robe over to her. "Mrs. Fish says it's okay, and even Phoebe doesn't argue with her very often."

They soon heard two women walking toward them, though they didn't sound very happy. In fact, they were arguing bitterly. The girls hunkered down in the back seat of the car at the sound of the loud, angry voices.

". . . and I'll pay that girl when I'm good and ready, Gilda! Furthermore, since you think I'm so selfish, I'm sure you certainly don't want to ride in the same car with me. I'll drive myself home. Here! Take this twenty dollar bill and call a taxi!" She opened the driver's side door and climbed in. A bill came sailing in after her.

"I don't want your money! You think you can control everyone with it, don't you? Well, not Gilda Fish!"

By now Katie and Alisha had slid from the back seat down

Stormy Fall

to the richly carpeted floor of the car. Alisha stared at Katie and mouthed the words, "What'll we do?"

Before Katie could answer, the front door slammed shut and the powerful engine roared to life.

Nurse Fish snatched the door handle. "You can't drive with that broken leg!" she shouted above the roar of the car engine.

"Just watch me!" With a clashing of gears the big Cadillac swung back and then forward out of the parking lot.

At the entrance to the main road, Katie felt the car making a right turn. They must be heading toward Mapleton. Suddenly, a blast of ear-shattering stereo music filled every inch of the car.

Alisha put her hands over her ears. "What *is* this?" she mouthed soundlessly.

Katie pulled the robe over their heads as she remembered back to her previous year's music-appreciation class. "Beethoven," she mouthed back, covering her ears with her hands, too. The thundering vibrations made her shake—or was it her fear of what would happen if Phoebe found them stowed away in her car?

She knew she didn't dare speak to the woman while she was driving down the sopping-wet hill like a maniac. There'd be a head-on collision for sure. Why had she ever thought she had to get her fifty dollars today? Right now, she'd happily abandon every penny of it just to be safely back in the church parking lot once more.

"Please, God," she tried to pray while the music blared and the car swerved down the hill. "Get us safely back to our homes!" Surely God could hear her prayer, even over the pulsing and pounding of Beethoven!

Stormy Fall

As if to say "Yes, Katie," the car began to slow down. Phoebe repeatedly honked her horn. Other cars must be daring to slow her speed.

Kerthump! Kerthump!

Alisha nudged Katie, and mouthed the words, "We're crossing the railroad tracks!"

Katie nodded. She gave silent thanks to God. At least they were going to downtown Mapleton and not onto the freeway.

The car was moving slower and slower now. Phoebe finally turned her stereo down a few decibels and the girls could begin to hear normal downtown sounds. They could feel the car stopping and starting up again at a couple of traffic lights. The car pulled to a stop and then eased forward a few yards. It nudged a curb and the sounds of the motor and stereo suddenly ceased.

Katie and Alisha both breathed their first breath of relief since beginning this mad race.

When Alisha started to rear up, Katie snatched her coat and shook her head. "Wait!" she whispered.

The door locks clicked open. Phoebe reached for her cane and climbed out of the car. Slamming the door shut, she and her cane clunked and clanked off down the sidewalk. Alisha and Katie heard a click.

After a few seconds had passed, Katie peered over the top of the back seat. "Ellison Simms's flower shop is only two stores down from here. She must have gone in there." Then, looking over at Alisha, she said, "Let's get out of here, Alisha. Take my word on this, we don't want to face the wrath of Phoebe!"

Alisha tried the door handle. It wouldn't budge. "Uh-oh. Katie, the door won't open!"

Stormy Fall

"Well, unlock it!" Katie said.

"There's no lock!" Alisha said. "I . . ."

At that moment Katie happened to look in the direction of Ellison Simms's flower shop again. The glass front door opened, and Phoebe stepped back out onto the sidewalk, accompanied by a young man in a green canvas apron who was carrying a big bouquet of red roses.

"She's coming back!" Katie said, ducking once more under the robe. Alisha joined her, and within a few seconds they heard the doors unlock and Phoebe open the driver's door. "Just put the flowers on the front seat," she said. The passenger door opened and the scent of roses drifted back to the girls.

When Phoebe clambered in and they heard the sound of footsteps walking away, Katie knew what she had to do. If she didn't, Phoebe might discover them halfway to her house and get them all killed.

Pushing the plaid robe aside, she held on to the back seat and pulled herself up. "Uh . . . hello, Mrs. Phillips!"

Phoebe screamed. Her car keys hit the front window. She looked back at Katie and screamed again, a screech as shrill and loud as the noon factory whistle back home in Sunnydale. "What are you two doing in my car?" she cried.

"Well, I only wanted to talk to you about the money you owe me. When you didn't come out of the church, Nurse Fish said . . ."

Phoebe practically stood up in the car. "You've been hiding in here since I left the church?"

"Well, Nurse Fish said we could sit in here and stay warm until you got back, and . . ."

Stormy Fall

Phoebe held up her hands. "Not another word! You're thieves, that's what you are! Why, I trusted you in my own home, Katie Barnes, and this is how you repay me. You and your sneaky friends!" She raised herself higher until she could see Alisha, who was shaking like a bobble-head doll.

A sudden change came over Phoebe. She smiled and calmly turned around, fastened her seat belt again and put the key in the ignition. "Do you girls know what I'm going to do now?" she asked in a smooth, silky voice. "I'm going to drive straight across town to the Mapleton Police Department and take you two inside. And what do you think they'll do?" Her face warped in fury and turned beet red. "Now sit down!" The girls quickly obeyed. With fumbling fingers they fastened their seat belts.

Phoebe started the car and glanced in her rearview mirror. Then, to Katie's surprise, she heard the car engine turn off again.

Phoebe sat there and tapped her long red fingernails on the steering wheel. "I've changed my mind, girls. Look out the back window."

Fear clutched Katie's heart and wouldn't let go. Slowly, she turned her head, and gasped.

"It's Mom and Dad! Alisha, Mom and Dad are here!"

Phoebe was smiling again. "Yes, your parents just pulled in behind us. Instead of turning you two over to the police, I'll turn you over to them! We'll see what they have to say about your behavior!"

But Alisha and Katie were ahead of her. Before Phoebe could step out with her cane, they were outside and dashing over to the old brown van. As Mom and Dad stepped out, they were grabbed in a double bear hug.

Stormy Fall

"Oh, Dad, it was just awful," moaned Katie. "Phoebe said she was going to take us to the police station and . . ."

"Whoa. Slow down, girls." Dad held her back so he could close the van door and walk over to Phoebe. "Now, what's this all about, Phoebe?"

"You tell me, Harvey." Phoebe hobbled up to them, pounding the pavement with her cane. "When you and Sarah decided to leave my apartment and move to this—this downtown slum, I warned you that you'd be sorry. This is no decent place to raise a family." She beckoned for the girls to join them. "And now I have proof. When I drove down to the flower shop after church today, I discovered these two girls *hiding* on the floor in my back seat! I have no idea what they were planning, but I feel I can safely say it was criminal." She stood there looking triumphant.

"Katie," Mom said in her sternest voice, "you'd better have a very good reason for doing such a thing."

"That's right," Dad agreed. "But first, Mrs. Phillips, I want to give you a big thank-you."

"What?"

"Yes." Dad beamed at her. "I want to thank you for bringing the girls safely from church." He turned his smile over to Katie and Alisha. "We got to worrying that there might have been a mix-up and they wouldn't have a ride home today. When we drove back to the church, Mrs. Fish said she thought they had ridden down here with you. If it hadn't been for you, they might have been stuck at the church."

"Did you hear what I said?" Phoebe cried. "This pair sneaked downtown in my car! I wasn't being nice. I mean . . . Well, of course I'm glad they're safely here. As a community we must look after our young people, but don't you both agree..."

"We surely do, Phoebe," Mom said. She grabbed Phoebe's hand and held it between her two hands. "And I want to join with Harvey in thanking you. You'll never know what a relief it is to see both girls standing here safe and sound."

Phoebe stood there with her mouth opening and shutting like a fish out of water. Finally, she pulled her hand loose from Mom's. "Very well," she said. "We'll call this matter closed. You take those two... girls with you, and I will go home. I have an important tea this afternoon. I'm glad I could relieve your mind, Sarah." She looked like she was in shock as she hobbled back to her new car. Dad quickly opened the door and helped her in. He put the cane inside and they all stepped back as Phoebe revved her engine.

"Oh, wait!" Katie said. She ran up to Phoebe's window. "My money, Mrs. Phillips; were you going to give me my money today?"

Phoebe turned off the car again. "Didn't I inform you I don't do business on Sunday?"

"Well, I just thought that after you bought those roses today, maybe you wouldn't mind?"

Phoebe glanced over at Dad. "Oh, very well," she said, anger once more flickering in her voice. She reached for her purse.

Katie held out her hands, and Phoebe dropped two twenties in them. "Uh, excuse me, but shouldn't that be $50?" Katie said.

Furiously, Phoebe tugged a ten dollar bill from her wallet and threw it at Katie. Without another word, she started the car, backed out, and sped off down the street.

Katie turned to face her folks. "Mom, Dad, we weren't trying to stow away. Mrs. Fish just told me to—"

"I know," Mom interrupted. "Mrs. Fish told us all about it when we drove her home today."

"But when Phoebe accused us of doing something horrible, you—"

"I was just playing along, Katie," Mom said. "I wanted to hear what happened, but I knew you hadn't done anything to Phoebe.

"Now, do you want us to drive you both over to Alisha's or do you want to stay with us this afternoon?"

"Well, my mom left us a nice lunch in the refrigerator," Alisha said, "and I've got some fun things planned. I personally think we should go to my house."

"Um, yeah, but if you wouldn't mind, Alisha," Katie said, "I think I'd rather walk to your place. I know it's pouring rain, but I've had enough car riding for one day."

They could still hear Dad's rumbling laugh as they turned the next corner to go to Alisha's house.

Chapter Eleven

Katie and Little Mike were the first ones up on Monday morning. Katie had gotten up early so she could finish her math homework. Since the rain was still pouring down, she invited Little Mike to come inside and keep her company.

Katie sat on the couch with her notebook open on her lap. Little Mike sat politely beside the couch with his head cocked to one side. The wet-dog smell was horribly strong, but whenever Katie reached down to pat his head, he thumped his tail happily on the floor.

Finally, Katie picked up her pencil and studied the last math problem. The pencil dropped from her fingers, however, when she heard the shaking and groaning of the ancient water pipes upstairs. Alex must be taking a bath. This could be her chance to check out his wallet and see what he was hiding from her. Setting her books on the couch, Katie got up and warned Little Mike to stay put.

Creeping up the stairs, she listened carefully. Yes, water was still running into the old claw-foot bathtub. She tapped lightly on Alex's bedroom door, then opened it a crack. Alex wasn't there, but his wallet lay in plain sight on top of his rumpled covers. Noiselessly, Katie slipped inside and closed the door.

Stormy Fall

She only felt a tiny bit of guilt as she picked up the wallet. After all, this was for Alex's own good. But a disappointing peek inside showed the wallet was empty—except for 23 cents in its coin compartment.

What had he done with that money? Spent it? Oh, she hoped not. Maybe he had it in the bathroom with him. Then again, maybe it was stashed away in his room.

She looked around. There wasn't much to see. Her gaze fell on three cardboard boxes holding all of his games and old toys. Katie knelt and pawed through each one, but found no money. She raised her head to listen again. She heard loud splashing in the bathroom.

There was no closet in the small bedroom. The only other possible hiding place would be his battered, paint-chipped chest of drawers.

Katie opened the drawers one by one. Junk, clean underwear, T-shirts, jeans, and cutoffs. But no money.

The bottom drawer stuck as Katie jerked it open. Inside, she spied Alex's comic book collection. Some of the old ones, he had inherited from Dad and Uncle Andy. Some he had found this summer while they were camping. A few were new. As Katie lifted each of the tattered books, she listened again for bathroom noises. The splashing stopped, and she heard the sound of water gurgling down the drain.

Katie quickly fumbled through each stack of books. Under the very last pile she spied a long envelope. With shaky fingers she opened it and saw—money! Thirty-five, fifty, sixty-three—over seventy dollars! As fast as possible, she returned the bills to the envelope and stuffed it back where she had found it, then she jumped up and almost ran from the room. She was closing her own bedroom door when she heard Alex come out of the bathroom.

Katie sagged against her door. She'd made it! But her good feeling only lasted a second. Then came dread as she remembered those bills she had stashed back in Alex's drawer. She and Alex had to have a talk!

She looked up. The little clock on her dresser warned her that time was racing by. Any heart-to-heart between her and Alex would have to take place this afternoon after school. Right now, there was going to be a race between Katie and the school bus!

Thankful that she'd taken her bath the night before, Katie hurriedly pulled on her long-sleeved brown-and-gold T-shirt and tan jeans. She ran a comb through her hair and rushed into the bathroom to brush her teeth.

At noon in the school cafeteria, Alisha sat down across from Katie. "What's wrong with you today, Katie? I don't think you spoke ten words on the bus this morning. Are you still thinking about yesterday?"

Katie shook her head while she sipped her carton of milk through a straw. "It's just a family problem. And don't worry . . ." She looked up into her friend's concerned face. ". . . I'll take care of it as soon as I get home this afternoon."

"Hey, girls, what's new since Saturday?" asked Tim as he and Shad stopped by their table. "Katie, did you ever get to talk to Phoebe yesterday?"

"Oh, yes." Katie smiled. "She and I finally got our business settled."

"Good." Tim and Shad sat down across from the girls. "Shad and I have been doing some brainstorming about our church crime."

Stormy Fall

Katie and Alisha nodded.

"Well, we all agree that Edith couldn't be the thief, right?" The girls nodded even harder.

"Then someone needs to find the real thief—or thieves. Maybe Edith's still alive and scared to come home because she thinks the police are blaming her."

Alisha held her hands out. "What can we do?"

Shad leaned forward. "You know, the thief could be someone right in our church—maybe even a teenager."

"None of the kids would do a thing like that!" protested Katie.

"I hope not," Shad replied. "But here's something we can do. We can be on the lookout for anyone—kids or adults—who suddenly has lots of money to spend."

Katie's baloney sandwich suddenly felt like lead in her stomach. She thought of the seventy dollars Alex had stashed away. Could her own little brother have taken part in this terrible crime? No, of course not! She knew Alex was better than that. Anyway, he and Skip were just ten-year-old kids. How could she even think such a thing? She would talk to her brother as soon as she got home this afternoon and he would prove he was innocent!

The afternoon didn't turn out as Katie had planned. When she got off the bus that day, Mom was waiting for her on the back porch.

"I'm so glad you're here, Katie. Alex's bus is late and I need someone to run to the store." She handed Katie two dollars. "I just started to mix up the cornbread for supper and I discovered I'm out of baking powder."

"Okay." Katie slid off her backpack. "Here's Alex's bus now. I'll see if he wants to go with me."

Stormy Fall

But Alex wasn't interested. "No way, Katie. I wasted all day at school, and I'm not about to waste more of it by walking to the store for baking powder." He tossed his backpack on the wet ground and ran across the yard to his dog. "Hey, Little Mike, did you miss me?"

Katie watched them. She should just grab Alex and make him tell her where he got that money! After all, she was still his big sister. Angrily, she zipped up her windbreaker and started off for the neighborhood convenience store.

The parking lot in front of the store was busy. There were cars at the gas pumps, cars parked in the spaces in front of the store, and cars just cruising through. Katie eased around them and entered the small building. A beep sounded as she walked inside.

The warm store felt good. She saw a line of customers waiting in front of the single cash register. After searching the shelves, she picked up a can of baking powder and joined the line.

"Hey, Katie, we meet again!"

Turning, Katie saw Shad Emery behind her in line, a loaf of bread in his hand. She laughed. "Your mom must have needed something from the store, too."

"Yeah," Shad said. "I walked in the door and walked right out again. Only this time, I have my cousin Charley with me. He's staying with us now, and I kind of watch out for him."

Katie looked around. "Is he in here?"

"That's him by the magazine rack."

Katie's eyes searched across the crowded store. She spied a lanky, stoop-shouldered teen with his back turned to them.

Stormy Fall

His black hair, done in dreadlocks, straggled below his denim-jacket collar. "Your cousin looks older than you, Shad. How come you have to watch after him?"

Shad heaved a sigh. "Charley's always getting into trouble." He lowered his voice. "He's been hanging out with a bad bunch of guys in Seattle. The family's afraid he'll end up in jail. Living with us is kind of his last chance."

"So is he Alisha's cousin also?"

"Nope. You see, Alisha's my cousin on Mom's side." He grinned. "I think she's pretty glad she's not related to Charley, too."

"Next!" called out the clerk. Katie turned to lay her can of baking powder and money on the counter.

"Hey, Katie, if you wait 'til I pay for this bread, I'll introduce you to Charley," Shad said. "He's starting to get antsy only having my family to talk to around here."

"I . . . guess so. Okay." Katie picked up her change, turned, and glanced back again at Shad's cousin. He was facing them now and looking straight at her—a cold, hard stare. Then his eyes got wide and a sneer twisted his face. He started toward her.

Katie gasped. The change slipped from her fingers and fell to the floor. She remembered meeting Shad's cousin before, and that memory chased icy chills up her back.

"Shad, I'd better run! I've got to hurry and get this baking powder to my mom," she told a surprised Shad. Scooping up the coins from the floor, she dashed for the door. The bell tinkled merrily.

Without looking back, Katie zigzagged across the busy parking lot. At 4:30 in the afternoon, most cars and pickups already had their lights on. Streetlights were on, too, making it easier for her to see through the rain as she sped home. When she was safely inside her own front gate, she finally looked behind her. No one was coming.

With a sigh of relief, she opened the back door into the cozy kitchen. Mom was waiting for her.

"I see it's raining again," said Mom. "Did you get the baking powder? Good! I'm just ready to put it in." She opened the lid, took off the inside paper, and began measuring baking powder into a big blue mixing bowl. "I didn't expect you back this soon, Katie."

"I hurried." Katie took off her wet windbreaker and sat down. "Shad Emery was at the store."

"Oh, really?" Mom said as she measured the salt.

"Yeah, he had his cousin Charley with him."

Mom nodded as she stirred. "I think the Emerys brought Charley with them to the Harvest Dinner."

"They did?" Katie sat there while a new idea crowded into her mind. "Mom, was Charley at the church the Sunday night after the dinner?"

"Goodness, I can't remember. Why all the questions anyway, Katie?"

Katie leaned forward. "Because I know that guy. Mom, do you remember back in Seattle this summer when three creepy, scary guys pulled a knife on Alex and me? How they forced us to go to this vacant lot and tried to rob us?"

"I remember that," Mom said. But she was peering out the window above the sink.

"Mom, are you listening to me? One of those three creeps was Shad's cousin Charley!"

Stormy Fall

But her mother wasn't listening. "Now who is that driving in here?" Her stirring spoon clattered into the mixing bowl. "I've got to answer the front door, honey." Without another word, she brushed right past Katie.

"What's wrong?" Katie pushed her chair back, jumped up, and hurried to look out the window. She saw car lights, but it was too dark to see the color of the vehicle. Then a dome light flicked on inside and two tall men in tan uniforms climbed out of the car. Before the doors closed, Katie saw an official emblem on the side of the car: Washington State Patrol.

Katie felt sick. They must be coming after Alex! They had learned about the money and thought he was part of the robbery. Katie had waited too long to talk to him.

"Katie, are those policemen going to put Alex in jail?" asked a small voice. Hannah had crept into the kitchen, her eyes round circles of fear.

"Hannah, where'd you come from?" whispered Katie.

"Mommy said I can't stay in the living room while the police talk to her and Alex. What's wrong?"

"Shhh!" Katie stood in the doorway and strained to listen. All she could hear were scraps of sentences. ". . . neighbor lady . . . assault . . . money . . . Skip . . ." in the patrolman's deep voice. Then there were a few soft, mumbled words from Alex.

"I knew it!" muttered Katie. "I knew Alex was in major trouble." And only his big sister could tell the police who the thief really was.

Finally, she couldn't wait any longer. Pushing Hannah back, she dashed down the short hallway to the living room. She stopped short. Two stern, official-looking patrolmen were sitting on straight-back wooden chairs. Mom and Alex sat across from them on the sagging old couch.

"Excuse me," blurted Katie. "But I may have important information about the case! The robbery at the church, I mean."

"Katie!" scolded Mom.

"Oh, that's all right, ma'am. We're always glad to get new information." One of the patrolmen smiled at Katie. "Go ahead, miss."

Katie took a deep breath. "First of all, my brother Alex is a good kid. No way would he ever steal anything—especially from a church. He even got a medal for five years perfect Sunday school attendance back home. And—and he loves animals!"

"Katie Barnes!" Her mom jumped up from the couch and marched across the room toward Katie. "These patrolmen aren't here because they suspect Alex of any crime!"

Katie stared at her. "They're not?"

"Of course not. Some of Skip's neighbors got into a family brawl while Alex was over there. The police hoped the boys might have seen something."

"I—I'm sorry," mumbled Katie. "I guess I messed things up." She turned and crept back toward the kitchen.

"Just a minute, Miss," said one of the patrolmen. "Did you say you had some evidence pertaining to the church robbery?"

Katie shook her head as she walked away. "No, I don't know anything. Sorry I wasted your time, sir."

As she stepped back into the kitchen, she could hear soft talking, then laughter.

They're laughing about me, she thought. *I made a joke out of myself by going in there. I'm glad I didn't say anything about Charley. I won't make any more statements unless I know what I'm talking about.*

Hannah must have gone upstairs, but Katie noticed the bowl of cornbread batter still sitting on the counter. Maybe she could do one thing right at least. She poured the yellow batter into a pan and popped it into the hot oven. As the cornbread baked, she stared through the kitchen window. By now the patrolmen were out at their car, and Mom and Alex were talking to them.

Another set of lights turned into the driveway, and Dad's brown van pulled up beside the patrol car. Soon all five of them were talking and nodding and shaking hands good-bye.

Dad was smiling when the three of them joined Katie in the kitchen. "Well, the state patrol told us our son was a polite and informative boy," he said. "And you, too, Katie." Dad grinned as he turned to her. "Though I'm sure you know, young lady, that folks usually don't interrupt officers of the law while they're interviewing someone."

Mom looked up at the wall clock. "Goodness, look at the time! It's past seven and we haven't eaten yet. The baked beans are all ready, and—oh no! I forgot to bake the cornbread! The batter is probably ruined!"

"It's okay, Mom," Katie said. "I put it in to bake."

"Oh, Katie," said Mom, "I don't know what we would ever do without you in this family. Although I can't imagine what made you think your own brother might be part of that church robbery."

Katie looked over at Alex, hoping he would explain about the money. But all he did was turn his face away.

Chapter Twelve

*W*hen the family finally sat down to supper that night, Alex loaded his plate with baked beans, coleslaw, and cornbread. "Man, it was cool talking to those policemen tonight," he said between bites. "I can hardly wait to tell Skip tomorrow." Obviously excited, he told his dad all about the interview.

Alex could never be that happy if he'd done something wrong, thought Katie. *So why doesn't he tell Mom and Dad about the money?* "Hey, Alex," she said as Mom began scraping plates, "I'll wash the dishes and you dry. Okay?"

"Katie, that sounds great," said Mom before Alex could open his mouth. "I think I'll go in the other room and put my feet up."

Dad and Hannah quickly followed her into the living room. Katie filled the sink with hot water and added detergent. "Okay, Alex, we're going to have a talk."

Alex scowled as he took a clean dishtowel from the drawer. "Yeah? What're we gonna talk about?"

"The money."

Alex's face looked blank. "What money?"

Katie faced him. "The seventy dollars you have stashed in the bottom drawer of your chest. Where'd it come from? And why haven't you told Mom and Dad about it?"

Stormy Fall

Katie angrily began plopping glasses into the dishwater. "You know I saw some of that money the day you were wrestling on the grass with your dog. And—I'll admit it—I found the rest of it this morning in your chest of drawers." She rinsed a glass and set it in the drainer. "Those patrolmen might not have been quite so jolly if they'd known about your secret stash."

Alex slammed the glass he'd just dried down on the counter. "You always have to play Nancy Drew, don't you. Even if it's your own brother! I haven't got any money. You can search the house from top to bottom and you won't find any 'stash.'" Angrily, he threw the dishtowel on the table. "Even in my bottom dresser drawer!" Turning, he stormed from the room.

Katie finished the dishes by herself. Later, she spread her books and papers out on the table and tried to catch up on her homework. Somehow, "participles" and "prepositions" didn't make much sense that night. Math problems were a lost cause, too. Finally, at eleven o'clock, she wearily closed and stacked her books, turned out the kitchen light, and went upstairs to bed.

In the dark bedroom, Katie quietly undressed and climbed into her pajamas so she wouldn't wake Hannah. As her eyes got used to the blackness, she looked across the room to her shelf of Nancy Drew books. Alex was right. It was time for her to quit trying to be Nancy, the girl detective. From now on, she vowed, she would leave police work up to the police.

It had been really stupid of her to suspect her own brother would be part of a gang that stole money. Even Shad's cousin, Charley . . . Katie pulled the covers up to her chin while she thought back to that scary night last summer.

Stormy Fall

Charley and two of his hoodlum buddies had grabbed Alex and her at knife point right on the streets of Seattle. Katie shivered at the memory. Terrified, she had tossed her wallet into some nearby blackberry bushes. Two of the creeps had dived after it, but not Charley. Instead, he had motioned for Alex and Katie to run off to safety.

Now she was ready to accuse him of the church robbery without any proof. Maybe Shad was right. Maybe his cousin just wanted to get a new start and lead a better life. Still, he'd sure looked scary when he spied her in the store that afternoon. . . . *Enough of this!* Katie turned on her side and tried to get to sleep.

Katie had just closed her eyes when Little Mike started to bark in the yard below. *Silly dog's afraid of his own shadow,* she thought. But on such a dark, rainy night, he wouldn't be able to see his shadow.

With a sigh, Katie threw back her covers and padded barefoot across the cold, vinyl-covered floor to the window. By now the rain was gone, but the fog was back and hiding everything behind a thick gray curtain. Little Mike kept up his barking. "Arf! Arf! Arf!"

A car was coming down the road. Maybe the car lights would convince that dog that nothing was out there this time of night. For an instant, as the car came near the house, the car lights cut through the fog. Little Mike stood stiff with his head high. Then Katie gasped as a figure out by the road darted behind the maple tree. It looked like a person wearing red, high-topped shoes! The next instant, all was fogged in again. Little Mike's barks slowly died away.

Katie stood at the window shaking. "I was imagining it,"

she whispered. "No one's out there. I'm just shaking because I'm cold." Nevertheless, she took a blanket from her bed, stood on a chair, and hung it over the curtain rod, hiding the window. Only then could she crawl back into bed and try to sleep.

By morning Katie could smile about her imaginary vision of a figure wearing red shoes. *It was just the fog,* she decided. *Fog distorts everything and makes it look crazy. If the fog would go away this fall, maybe all the problems would go away, too.*

On the school bus that morning, Alisha had her nose buried in her Lit book. Katie yawned. She leaned across the aisle to Tim. "It's a wonder we don't have all kinds of crimes around here with all this horrible fog and dumb, ugly rain. People could get away with *anything.*"

"Katie, fog is nothing but a big mass of tiny drops of water suspended in the air just above the ground." He grinned. "The sun and moon and stars are still up in the sky, just like always."

Katie tried not to look too bored as Tim's voice droned on.

Alisha looked up from her book. "Tim, I think you already know more about weather than we could ever want to."

Tim's grin spread. "Yeah, I'm thinking about being a weatherman someday—a meteorologist. I think it'd be a 'cool' job. That's a weather joke, in case you didn't catch it."

Katie and Alisha looked at each other and raised their eyebrows. Katie decided it was time to change the subject, and looked around. "Where's Shad this morning?"

"Oh, the poor guy's getting a couple of fillings at the dentist. His mom'll bring him to school later," Alisha said.

Katie looked out the window as their bus rumbled by the church building. She turned to Tim again. "You deliver

Stormy Fall

newspapers every day. Does the paper say the police are still looking into the church robbery, or are they just going to blame poor Edith?"

Tim shrugged. "The papers haven't been saying much lately. They *did* put in an article about our finding Edith's cap and those checks. I get the feeling a lot of people figure Edith was the thief, and that she drowned in the river while she was trying to get away."

Katie nodded. "I wonder what the police'd think if they knew someone who had been in trouble with the Seattle police was at the Harvest Dinner?"

Tim looked at her curiously. "Do you know something I don't, Katie?"

"Not really." Katie leaned back in her seat and was silent until the bus pulled up at Benjamin Franklin Junior High.

Mark Gomez stepped off the bus right behind Tim.

"Hey, guys, don't forget—tomorrow night's pizza night at youth meeting. Oh man, I can't wait!" Mark called out to Tim and the girls.

"Yeah, Shad told me about the pizza," Tim said. "Don't worry, we'll be there. And we won't be late. Otherwise, you probably wouldn't even leave us a scrap of crust."

"Especially when the pizza is delivered hot from Pizza Pete's," Alisha agreed. "They've got the best pepperoni pizza in King County!"

It was foggy again Wednesday evening. When Dad drove Katie into the parking lot, he left the van lights on while she started up the sidewalk. "I don't want you to get lost along the way," he said with a smile.

"Don't worry, Dad," Katie said, climbing out of the van. "I can smell those pizzas from here. I could find them if I was blind and had only one nostril!" She could still hear Dad chuckling as he drove out of the parking lot. Then Katie turned and followed her nose.

Sue Wong was waiting for her when she walked into the meeting room. "Katie! I've been trying to catch you all week at school. It seemed like every time I got close, you disappeared."

"Yeah, well, I've been pretty busy." Katie didn't return Sue's smile. "What did you want, Sue?"

"I was wondering if you'd like to be worship chairman of the youth group. What do you think?"

"No, I don't think so. Like I said, Sue, I'm pretty busy."

"Oh, please, Katie!" begged Sue. "You'd be just perfect as chairman. I know you would."

Katie pushed past Sue. "That's the same thing you told me after I tried out for cheerleader, Sue. Then you voted against me."

Sue was silent for a moment. Then she walked over to Katie, firmly took her arm, and turned Katie around to face her. "Is that what's been wrong with you lately, Katie? I've been wondering. Yes, I voted against you for cheerleader. Do you want to know why?"

"I guess," Katie said.

"Okay, it was because I saw you shooting hoops after our youth meeting one night. You're good, Katie! You shot those baskets like a pro!"

Katie stared at her. "Yeah, I've played a lot of basketball. So what?"

"So, you probably didn't know the school is going to start a girls basketball team this year, did you? They just made the decision final recently. You belong on that team, Katie!"

"Let me get this straight," Katie said. "You voted against me for cheerleader so I could try out for the girls basketball team?"

"Exactly! You're too good at basketball to be a cheerleader. You belong on one of the teams we're cheering for!"

"And you didn't vote against me because my family lives in Lower Mapleton or because we're poor?" Katie persisted.

"Of course not. What does that have to do with anything?"

"Nothing at all," replied Katie. "Oh, thank you, Sue!" She grabbed the taller girl's hands and swung her around. "This means so much to me!" She stopped when they nearly bumped into Gwen Van Switt, who had been eavesdropping throughout the conversation. "Did you hear that, Gwen? I'm going to try out for basketball! Isn't that cool?"

"Oh, yes! Really cool!" agreed Gwen. "I always said, Katie, that if Sue voted against you for cheerleader, she would probably have a better reason than that you're a little clumsy when you're jumping."

Katie smiled at her. "I'm so happy tonight, Gwen, that even *you* can't upset me. Now I'm going to eat pizza!"

The best news of the evening, however, came after the pizza, a short business meeting, and the study lesson on the book of James. As everyone was getting ready to leave, Pastor Miller slipped into the room and spoke quietly to the Kippers.

Stormy Fall

"Good news!" Ed held up his hand for silence. "Pastor Miller just told us that Stella Tootle has been moving around a lot and the doctors think she may soon regain consciousness. Maybe at last we'll learn what happened that terrible night of the accident."

"Come on, guys!" Sue held out both hands. "Let's have a circle of prayer and thank the Lord."

After the meeting, only Shad braved the cold and hurried out to the basketball hoop with his ball. He dribbled a few times, then easily shot the ball into the hoop. "Hey, Ace," he called to Katie when she walked by. "Wanna take a shot?"

"No, thanks." Katie laughed. "My fingers are so cold, they'd probably break off if I picked up that basketball." She stood there shivering while she watched Shad make a couple more baskets. "Hey, Shad, how's your cousin Charley getting along?" she finally asked.

Shad dribbled the ball a few times. "Really good, I think. He enrolled in high school this week." He shot one more basket, then walked over to Katie. "You know, Katie, he told me he's thinking about becoming a Christian. Man, that'd be so awesome." He and Katie started walking out to his dad's van. "His two best friends weren't so lucky, though. One of them was killed in a robbery a week or two back and the other one's in jail. Charley's taking it pretty hard. Would you mind praying for him, Katie?"

"Sure," Katie said. It was all she could do.

By the time Katie got home she was so excited, she feared she would lie awake all night and stare at the ceiling. It was good to know that Sue was still her friend, that she would probably be playing basketball this winter, and, best of all, that Stella was getting better. Now if only Edith would return. And if only she could be as certain as Shad that his cousin was really trying to make a new life for himself.

"Katie," whispered a small voice when Katie entered her bedroom.

Katie looked over toward Hannah. "Are you still awake? It's late, Hannah."

Hannah sniffled. "I couldn't sleep 'til you got here." She sat up in bed. "Katie, I saw a bad guy!"

Katie sat up on the edge of her bed. "Hannah, what are you talking about? Do you mean you saw someone on TV?"

"No! I looked out the window, and I saw him. He was down by the road and he was a giant! And he was purple and he had on red shoes!"

Katie could feel herself trembling as she moved over and sat on the edge of her little sister's bed. "I think it was just a bad dream, hon. No purple giant would dare come around here. Everything's going to be fine. I'll sit right here on your bed until you fall asleep."

Katie sat on the bed for a long time before Hannah's eyes finally closed. Then she crept over to the window and cautiously looked out across the yard. Everything was still. Little Mike was silent. A tiny breeze ruffled the branches of the maple out by the road. "That's all it was," whispered Katie. "Last night and tonight both. Just the wind and the fog. Definitely not some purple giant with red shoes." Nevertheless, Katie hung her blanket over the window again.

Chapter Thirteen

*F*riday evening, Mom went to the closet and brought out Katie's thin windbreaker. "Katie, tonight you and I are going shopping for a winter coat. The weatherman says we're in for a real storm, and you're still walking around in goose bumps."

Katie shook her head. "I don't think so, Mom. The guys say I can't buy a winter coat for fifty dollars."

Her mom smiled. "You can at the store I'm thinking about. Now, grab your windbreaker and let's go. Just the two of us."

A few minutes later, they pulled in at a brightly lit store on the far side of town. "Bargain Village" read the overhead sign.

"Mom, this is a secondhand store!" yelped Katie. "I'm not going to wear a used coat!"

"Let's just look," coaxed Mom.

The cars had thinned out in the parking lot as they left the store. Katie was wearing her "new" coat and keeping her head low in case she saw someone she knew.

"This is so humiliating," she said. "Buying a secondhand coat is just what the snobs up on the hill would expect me to do."

"Katie, that coat looks practically new," Mom said. "One of the women at work told me about this store—said she buys almost all her family's clothes here." She looked over at Katie. "That lavender color looks real good on you, hon. I always loved lavender. White and lavender were my wedding colors. Goodness, to think that was fifteen years ago tomorrow. How time flies." She unlocked the van.

Katie began to feel ashamed. Here she was, yammering on about wearing a used coat, and she'd forgotten all about her parents' anniversary—for a second time. At least she still had a little money left. She pulled out her wallet. "Here, Mom." She held out her last ten dollar bill. "I have this money left from buying my coat. I want you and Dad to use it to help you go somewhere for your anniversary."

Mom put the bill back in Katie's hand. "You worked too hard for this money, Katie. No, your dad and I will celebrate with a nice family dinner at home."

Katie thought hard. "Okay, we'll celebrate at home, but we three kids will cook the dinner. It'll be our present to you."

"Now that's an offer we can't refuse," Mom said with a big smile.

Later, after they got home, Katie beckoned Alex and Hannah out to the kitchen. "I'm sure you remember that tomorrow is Mom and Dad's anniversary. Right, Alex?"

Alex looked blank. "It is? Just foolin' around—I remember. So, what have you got in mind, Katie?"

"Well, we kids are going to cook a special dinner for them. I want you both to be here tomorrow afternoon. Okay?"

"Okay!" Hannah said. "I'll make a pretty paper chain for decoration, like we do at kindergarten."

Stormy Fall

"Make it lavender and white. Those were Mom and Dad's wedding colors." Katie looked over at Alex. "Now, how about you?"

"Me? Uh, yeah, sure, I'll be here to help."

But when Saturday afternoon came, Alex was nowhere to be seen. Once again, he was up at Skip's house.

"This is going to be Mommy and Daddy's best anniversary ever, isn't it?" Hannah pasted another strip of paper onto a lavender-and-white paper chain that already stretched the length of the kitchen floor.

"I hope so. This is their fifteenth anniversary and it *should* be special." Katie added a can of tomato sauce to a gooey mixture of ground beef, dry oatmeal, and raw eggs. She stooped to read the recipe on the side of the round oatmeal box. "One-fourth cup chopped onions. Yuck! I hate chopping onions! Oh, well, I guess. Anything for Mom and Dad."

Hannah dropped the scissors and paper on the table and came over to the counter to watch her big sister. "I wanna help fix the food, Katie. I'm tired of pasting."

Katie looked around for something else a five-year-old could do without ruining everything. "Okay, Hannah, there's a bowl of frosting on the counter. Wash your hands and take it over to the table. You can frost the cake."

"Yaaay!" Hannah pulled a stool over to the kitchen sink and scrubbed her hands.

"Now don't go adding any more food coloring to that frosting like you did last time," Katie said.

"I won't," promised Hannah. "Katie, why isn't Alex helping us? He said he would!"

"I guess he thinks Skip's more important than helping."

Katie put the meatloaf mixture into a baking pan and shaped it. "But he promised he'd at least be home in time for dinner." She turned to put the meatloaf in the oven and started peeling potatoes. "He sure better be."

Hannah began spreading white frosting on the chocolate cake. Katie cringed at the chocolate crumbs that were mixed into the white frosting.

Katie got the best white tablecloth from a drawer and spread it on the table. Standing back to look at it, she frowned. Something was missing.

"There's no flowers on the table," Hannah said.

"Flowers! I should have thought of that." Katie looked around. "Well, we'll just have to make do with Mom's ivy plant." She placed the flowing green plant in the center of the tablecloth and stood back. "It still needs something. I'm going to get the yellow candles from the living room." The candles were exactly what the table needed.

When Mom and Dad drove in after shopping for groceries, Mom put on her best blue lace dress and Dad looked stiff and uncomfortable in his suit. Although the family sat and waited, Alex hadn't come home yet.

"Well, we better go ahead and eat or dinner will be ruined," Katie said. She went into the kitchen, smoothed the tablecloth, and lit the candles. "Dinner is ready," she called as she clicked off the kitchen lights.

"Oh, my, this is just the nicest anniversary dinner we've ever had," Mom said as she entered the kitchen.

"And look at that meatloaf!" exclaimed Dad. "Why, we wouldn't have such a grand meal if we'd gone to the best restaurant in Seattle." He held Mom's chair for her as she sat down.

Stormy Fall

Mom smiled at the two girls. "I'm sure it'll taste every bit as good as it looks. And that beautiful blue cake! I've never seen one quite like that."

Katie scowled at beaming Hannah. "Yeah, Hannah got into the blue food coloring while I was out of the kitchen for a minute."

"Well that's just fine," said Mom. "I've always liked royal blue."

Just as Dad was ready to say grace, car lights flashed through the kitchen window and a car door slammed.

"It sounds like Alex finally made it," Katie said. "About time."

They all turned to watch as the kitchen door opened and Alex slunk in. His curly hair was standing on end, and his round face was flushed. "Sorry I'm late," he mumbled. "Something came up." He looked anxiously back at the door.

"We'll talk about this later, young man." Dad's usually jolly face was stern. "Right now, sit down and help us eat this great anniversary dinner."

But before Alex could sit, they heard a loud pounding at the door.

"Who could *that* be?" Dad jumped up and started for the door.

"Wait, Dad!" Alex said. But his dad had already swung the door open. Mom, Hannah, and Katie sat frozen at the table, their mouths as wide open as the door.

"Come on in, guys!" said Alex with a grin. Everyone stared as Skip Young, his dad, and another boy walked single file into the kitchen. Each one was carrying a cardboard box. Alex snatched the biggest box from Mr. Young and struggled to put it on the table. Katie hurriedly pushed the dishes to one side.

"Happy anniversary, Mom and Dad!" Alex grinned at his folks. The two boys set down the other boxes.

Dad looked into the big box. "Why, Alex, this looks like a computer!"

"Yep, and a monitor and keyboard and everything."

"Oh, Alex!" Mom got her voice back. "Where did they come from? How did you ever afford something like this?"

"I earned the money," said Alex proudly. "That's why I've been going up to Skip's house so much. It wasn't just for our geography project. You see, Skip's neighbor owns an electronics shop, and he has a whole basement full of old computers. He fixes 'em and sells 'em cheap. He's been letting me work out the price of this one. It's kind of old, but it works fine. I cleaned out his garage. I washed and waxed his two cars. I ran errands." Alex stopped to catch his breath.

"Your boy's worked like a trooper," said Mr. Young. "He even walked our neighbor's dog."

"Why, Alex, that's wonderful!" said Mom. She turned to Mr. Young. "And thank you for helping to make this possible." She smiled at the strange boy. "You must be Skip's older brother."

"Joe Young Jr.," the boy said.

"How about joining us for dinner?" Dad said.

"No, we won't intrude. This is your special night," said Mr. Young, starting toward the door.

"All right, Joe. We'll invite you guys another day," promised Dad.

"Maybe Thanksgiving!" Mom quickly agreed.

After the Young family left for home, Katie moved the dishes back in place and turned off the lights. With the complete family now sitting at the table, they bowed their heads and thanked God for all of their blessings, especially this anniversary.

After dinner, Katie insisted that her mom and dad go into the living room while the kids cleaned up the kitchen.

"Alex, why didn't you tell me you were earning money to buy a computer?" Katie said. "You know how worried I've been since I saw those bills in your pocket!"

"I didn't want to tell you. I knew you'd blab," said Alex. "This was my secret project that I was doing all by myself. If I'd told you, it wouldn't have been my secret anymore. It worked, too!" He laughed. "Man, you should have seen your faces when you saw I had a computer in those boxes!"

"Oh, it worked, all right," agreed Katie. "You had me thinking you were part of a gang of crooks that robbed churches."

"Well, that's what you get for always sneaking around like Nancy Drew," kidded Alex. He hung his wet dishtowel on the rack. "Hey, speaking of crooks, Katie, d'you remember those three that used a knife on you and me to scare us last summer in Seattle?"

Katie looked quickly over at him. "Yeah, so what?"

Alex folded his arms and leaned back against the cupboard. "So I thought I saw one of them Sunday night after church."

"Oh, really?"

"Yeah, he looked just like one of them. He wasn't, though. He's Shad Emery's cousin, and he's real cool. He's gonna help some of us learn to play football next summer." Alex grinned. "Man, I'm glad I didn't open my big mouth to that guy. Only a dummy would think a neat family like the Emerys could have a crook for a relative."

"Only a dummy," agreed Katie.

At ten o'clock that night Hannah was finally coaxed into going up to bed, but the rest of the family gathered around the computer until nearly midnight.

"All right, everybody," said Mom. "I think we all agree this has been one special day. But now it's time to turn off the computer and go to bed." No one argued.

When Katie slipped into her room, she got ready for bed in the dark. She took one peek out the window. Everything was peaceful. Not a leaf stirred. She glanced at the blanket on the foot of the bed, but left it there.

Climbing into bed, she pulled the covers up to her chin. What a great day this had been. They had given Mom and Dad a happy anniversary, but even more important, she had her brother back once more. Tonight had felt like old times. *I'll never be cross or crabby or suspicious of Alex or Hannah again,* she vowed to herself. She was in the middle of thanking God for her wonderful family, when she drifted off to sleep.

"Katie! Katie! Wake up!" Groggily, Katie struggled to open her eyes. Hannah was bouncing up and down on her bed.

"Go on, Hannah. Quit bouncing on the bed and let me sleep."

"No, Katie! Mama said for me to wake you up and tell you it's already 8:30! We have to go to Sunday school."

Katie turned, looked at the clock, and groaned. "All right. If you quit bugging me, I'll get up. I want to take a bath and wash my hair." She pushed Hannah off the bed and threw the covers back.

"You can't take a bath. Alex took his bath and used up all the hot water."

"Oh, great," grumbled Katie.

Stormy Fall

The only good thing about Sunday morning was that she had a warm coat to wear to church. She met Alisha right outside their classroom.

"Katie, you got your new coat!" said Alisha. "It looks so nice and warm. Where did you buy it?"

"Uh, at a shop one of Mom's friends told her about."

"Do they have any more like that? I'm going to need a new coat, too."

"Well, I think this was pretty much the only coat just like this. Sorry." But Katie couldn't keep the secret from her good friend for long. She sighed and leaned close. "I bought this coat secondhand from Bargain Village," she whispered. "Please don't tell anyone else."

"Oh, don't worry, Katie," Alisha whispered back. "Lots of kids buy used clothes from Bargain Village. It's a cool thing to do." She opened the door to their classroom.

"Yeah, but it's not so cool when that's all you can afford." Katie followed Alisha into the room and sat down beside her. "Anyway," she spoke softly, "since this jacket only cost $40, I still have the ten I got from Phoebe." She pulled the bill from her wallet and waved it in front of Alisha. "We can go have a soda this afternoon."

"Wow, Katie, you're giving money away? Thanks!" teased Shad, who was sitting behind them. His long arm reached over her shoulder and he snatched the ten dollar bill. He handed it to Tim. "Here, Tim, Katie's passing out free money!"

"Hey, thanks!" Tim said.

"You two clowns give my money back!" Katie lurched after the ten dollar bill, knocking over a folding chair.

Tim laughed as he passed the bill back to her. "Take it, please, before you knock down our whole classroom!" But just as Katie's fingers touched the bill, Tim snatched it back. "Wait a minute," he said. His smile faded as he looked closely at the bill. "Do you remember where you got this, Katie?"

"Sure. Phoebe gave it to me last Sunday. Why?"

"All right, kids, let's settle down!" Mrs. Ford, their teacher tapped on the table. "It's ten o'clock and time to begin class."

"We need to talk!" he whispered. "I have to leave right after Sunday school, but I'll see you on the bus tomorrow morning. Please, please, don't spend that money before then!"

Chapter Fourteen

But why? What's wrong?" asked Katie. Kids sitting nearby frowned at her as Mrs. Ford started praying. Finally, she tucked the bill safely back in her wallet. Oh, well, she'd just have to wait until tomorrow.

Waiting had never been easy for Katie. During the services at church and throughout the long Sunday, she fidgeted and wondered. Should she call Tim and demand an answer? Several times she walked over to the kitchen wall phone, but stopped before dialing. No, if this was a really big secret, Tim might not want his younger brothers and sisters listening to him talk.

While lying in bed that night, Katie tried to figure out how a ten dollar bill could be so important. But her mind stayed blank, so she had to settle on going to sleep.

Monday morning, she was waiting out at her bus stop ten minutes before the bus slowed to a stop with a hissing of air brakes and belching of diesel smoke.

"Well, well," Judd greeted her. "You're on time for once!"

"Back here, Katie!" called Alisha. "Tim and I swapped seats so you two can have your talk." She sat back down beside Shad.

"So, what's this all about, Tim?" Katie asked as she sat

down. She took the folded ten dollar bill from her wallet and handed it to him.

"Look!" Tim held the bill out and pointed to the oval picture of Alexander Hamilton etched on one side.

"What about it?" Then Katie looked closer. On one side of the image someone had printed *Sean*. On the other side was printed *Patrick*. "Sean Patrick? Who's that?"

"He's my uncle. That was his lucky ten dollar bill," said Tim. "His best friend gave it to him when they were both in the navy. He printed Uncle Sean's name on it."

Katie stared at the green bill. "Yeah, it's a coincidence, all right. I mean, Phoebe having this bill that had once belonged to your uncle. But I don't see . . ."

"It's more of a coincidence than that." Tim was looking serious. "You see, Uncle Sean donated his lucky ten dollar bill to our Harvest Dinner offering. It would have been part of the money that was stolen the very next night!"

"Now wait a minute, Tim. It sounds like you're accusing Phoebe of being in on that robbery."

"No, Katie, I'm not accusing her of anything. I'm just saying that if she remembers where she got that bill, it might really help the police." He handed the bill back to Katie. "Here, this is yours. It's up to you to decide what to do with it."

"Honestly, Tim, I don't know what to do with it." She looked over at the tall red-haired boy. "What would you do?"

Tim slumped in the seat with his arms folded across his chest. "Well," he said finally, "I think I'd talk to Phoebe about the bill. First, though, I'd pray for God to give me the right words to say. With Phoebe Phillips, that won't be easy."

"Just what I was thinking," said Katie. Both of them sat

Stormy Fall

without talking until the bus pulled up at Ben Franklin Junior High.

Alisha caught up with Katie as the bus kids walked into the school building. "Is everything okay, Katie? It sounded like you and Tim were doing some heavy talking."

"Heavy is right," Katie said. "Alisha, we discovered that the ten dollar bill Phoebe gave me last Sunday is a specially marked one Tim's uncle had put into the Harvest Dinner offering."

Alisha's mouth fell open. "Well, how'd Phoebe get it? Oh, Katie, do you think . . . I mean, is it possible . . . No. It couldn't be! What are you going to do? Is there any way I can help?"

"I'm glad you asked that," Katie said, "because I'm thinking of borrowing a bike and riding up to Phoebe's house to talk to her."

"And you want to borrow my bike? Sure, Katie, I'll be glad to loan it to you."

"Oh, no, I'm going to try to borrow Janie's bike. I was hoping you'd come with me, Alisha." Katie couldn't help grinning at the horrified look on her friend's face.

"*Me?* After that terrible ride we had with her last week? I don't think so, Katie." Alisha looked at Katie. "I'm a coward, aren't I?" She sighed. "Okay, if you decide to ride a bike up there, I'll go with you."

"I'll let you know tonight," Katie said as they split up to go to their first classes.

∽

After supper that evening, Katie went up to her room. Her bed creaked as she sat down on the edge of it. "What should

133

Stormy Fall

I do, God?" she whispered. "Surely Phoebe didn't have anything to do with this, right? I mean, she's a fine Christian lady. I know I need to talk to her, Lord, but her temper! What should I do? What should I say?"

Sighing, Katie stood up and walked across the cracked linoleum floor to the window. In the gathering darkness the rain pounded against the window panes. Katie pressed her nose against the glass and looked down.

She heard the front door close and saw her dad walk down the steps and across to the edge of the yard. He didn't even seem to notice the rain. Slowly, his tall, stooped figure moved along the yard, his hands jammed in the pockets of his denim work jacket. Curious, Katie pulled on her coat and made her way down the stairs and out the front door. She pulled her hood over her hair.

"Hey, Dad!" she called. "Why are you walking around in the rain? Did you lose something?"

"What? Oh, no, Katie, I'm just stepping the place off. It's something my dad used to do when I was a little boy. Every fall, he'd walk around the outside edges of our little farm, figuring out what crops had done best. He'd decide what to plant—and where to plant it—the next year."

Katie walked along, keeping step with her dad. "So now you're figuring what you want to plant next spring?"

Dad chuckled. "Oh, I won't be planting any corn fields, but I think over there on the south side . . ."—he pointed—"would be a good garden spot." He looked down the road. "Hmm. I wonder who's walking this way with a flashlight?" Katie spun around and saw a blurred, wavering circle of light.

"Katie? Is that you?" called a familiar voice.

Stormy Fall

"You know very well it's me, Tim Reilly. You're standing right in front of our place. What are you doing out here in the rain?"

"Looking for Megan's old cat, Rusty. He's been missing all day, and she's worried. You folks haven't seen him around here, have you?"

"I don't think so," said Dad. "Seems like a cat would stay close to home on a night like this."

"Yeah, but old Rusty's a wanderer." Tim swept his light across the road. "I guess I'll go scope out that grove of alder trees across the road. Maybe Rusty got himself stuck up a tree. Megan'll bawl her eyes out if we don't find him."

"I'll help you, Tim," volunteered Katie. "Is it okay, Dad?"

"I don't know about that, Katie. It's almost completely dark, and it's raining pretty hard. I don't want you getting lost."

"She'll be okay, Mr. Barnes," promised Tim. "I know that little grove like the back of my hand. Some of us guys camp out there every summer."

"Well, all right." Dad glanced at the luminous dial on his wristwatch. "Ten minutes, Katie, or I'll come to check on you."

"I promise we'll be right back," said Katie. "Honestly," she muttered as Tim lit their steps down the driveway. "What does Dad think could happen practically in my own front yard?"

Tim laughed. "He probably doesn't want you running around in the dark with a fourteen-year-old boy."

"Ha," said Katie. "Dad should know by now that I can take care of myself where any boy is concerned."

Stormy Fall

Gravel crunched under their feet as they trudged to the road. "So, Katie, what did you decide to do about your ten dollar bill?" asked Tim.

As usual, Katie had to take long strides to keep up with Tim. "I think Alisha and I will ride bikes up there tomorrow afternoon so I can talk to Phoebe."

"Ride bikes?" Tim almost dropped his flashlight. "That's more than five miles! And look at this weather."

Katie shrugged. "What else can I do? Phoebe did a lot for my family last summer. I don't want to get my folks involved in this unless I have to."

They both looked up and down the road for cars, then hurried across to the small grove of trees. By now a wind had come up and the trees were bending low.

Tim aimed his flashlight beam up into the bare limbs. "Here, kitty, kitty, kitty . . ." He turned back to Katie. "I've got an idea for you. The church trustees are having a meeting over at Good Sam House Wednesday evening. Phoebe wouldn't miss that for anything. Maybe you could talk to her there."

"Hey, that's great! I could leave the youth meeting a little early and go right next door and talk to Phoebe." Katie laughed. "Alisha will love that. I think she dreaded facing Phoebe again more than she dreaded that long bike ride up the hill."

"No wonder." Tim peered up into the trees again. "I don't think Rusty's up there. Here." He handed the flashlight to Katie. "You stay under these trees. I can see well enough to go check out that brushy slope." He crept away in the darkness. Katie was left alone.

Stormy Fall

Soon she could no longer hear Tim crashing through the underbrush behind her. The only sounds around her in the rainy darkness were her own teeth chattering and the wind blowing. By now the rain was falling so hard, Katie couldn't even see the lights of her own home across the way. When she aimed the flashlight beam up into the tree limbs, they were swaying violently and looked like ghostly figures.

Suddenly there was a thunderous crash and a huge branch fell in front of her.

Katie gasped. Her voice quivered as she called out, "Here, Rusty, kitty! Here, kitty!"

"Meerow!"

Katie jumped. "R-Rusty?"

"Meerow! Meerow!"

The poor cat must have a terrible cold. Very slowly, Katie followed the harsh wailing behind the trees. Suddenly, she tripped over a big tree root and fell flat onto the cold wet ground. The flashlight rolled from her hand. Katie frantically reached for it, only to feel her wrist grabbed by a strong hand. Her heart thudded. "Tim, is that you?"

Another hand clamped over her mouth. Inches away, the beam of the flashlight shone through the weeds and lit the ankles and feet of her attacker. They were huge feet, and they wore muddy red hiking boots.

Chapter Fifteen

Desperately, Katie tried to wrestle free from the strong hands. They only clutched tighter. She couldn't breathe.

"Will you keep your mouth shut if I take my hand away?" asked a raspy voice.

Katie nodded. The hand pulled away.

"Help, Da—" The hand clamped off her words.

She began to twist and kick again. Finally, with her free left hand, she felt for the flashlight. Stretching her fingers, she managed to grasp it and swing the blinding rays straight into her attacker's eyes.

In the sudden brightness, she stared up into the angry, dark face of her old enemy Charley, who was dressed in a purple jogging suit. "Yeow! You're blinding me!" He let loose of Katie's wrist.

"I thought it was you, you big bully! I recognized you in the convenience store, too. Now you're snooping around our place at night, scaring my little sister out of her wits!" Katie was so mad, she balled her hands into fists and reached up to sock him in the face.

"Hey, cut it out!" Charley held his hands in front of his face. "I recognized you right away, too. You and your big mouth!"

"You're the thief who robbed our church, too, aren't you?" She swung her fist again, and Charley dodged it just in time.

"It figures you'd blame me for that. Some crook sneaks in and steals from your church and right away you're ready to accuse me. It doesn't matter, though," he added bitterly. "Cops already knew I have a record in Seattle, so they checked on me the next day." He pulled back into the darkness. "Now get that light away!"

Katie lowered the flashlight. The wind almost tore it from her hand. "Wait a minute. Are you trying to weasel out of the robbery?"

"I don't have to 'weasel out,' 'cause I didn't do it. And with someone like you in the neighborhood, I'm glad I had an alibi! Shad and his folks will vouch that I was asleep on the top bunk of Shad's bunk bed all night long that night."

"Ha! Likely story! If you're so innocent, you've got nothing to worry about, so why keep snooping around my place at night?"

"Would you have talked to me if you'd seen me coming?" Charley's shoulders slumped. He jammed his big hands into the pockets of his pants. "I guess I wanted to scare you a little bit so you'd keep quiet about our meeting last summer. I wasn't going to hurt you. Hey, if it hadn't been for me, ol' Slink might have cut a couple of slash marks right across your face back in Seattle."

Katie shivered at the thought. "So what do you want to talk to me about?"

Charley blinked away raindrops. "I was only going to ask you not to mess things up for me here in Mapleton. I got a new chance out here, if you don't blab to everyone about Seattle." He paused. "Well, what do you say?"

Stormy Fall

But before Katie could answer, they heard a rustling, crashing noise behind them. Tim burst out of the underbrush with a big, wet orange cat perched on his shoulder. "The next time you take off in a rainstorm, Rusty, you can find your own way home," Tim scolded. He blinked as he peered at the two of them. "Well, hey, Charley. Where'd you come from? Don't tell me you were out jogging in this storm." He shifted the heavy cat to his other shoulder.

"Yeah. We joggers run in all kinds of weather." Charley shook his black afro, and water sprayed everywhere. "I saw Katie calling for the cat. Thought I'd see if she needed any help."

"So I guess you guys know each other, then?"

"Well, we were kind of getting acquainted while we waited for you," replied Katie.

"Charley's living here with Shad's family now. He's going to be the next star quarterback of Mapleton High." Katie turned to the tall figure, who was waiting in the shadows. She frowned briefly, then sighed, forcing a smile on her face. "Welcome to Mapleton, Charley. I hope you like it here."

"Thanks," said Charley. It was the first time Katie had ever seen him smile.

"Katie, is everything okay over there?" called Dad from across the road.

"Everything's fine, Dad," Katie shouted back. "I'll be right with you."

Later that night, Katie stood in front of her bedroom mirror, brushing her straight, shoulder-length hair. In the reflection she saw Hannah sitting up in bed watching her.

"Katie, would you hang the blanket over the window tonight so we won't have to see the giant?"

Stormy Fall

"There's no giant out there, Hannah. Only wind and rain. And I don't think anyone will be bothering us again." Katie walked over and pulled the covers up to Hannah's small chin. "Anyway, winter's coming and I want to use that blanket to keep warm. Go to sleep now."

In a few minutes, with Hannah fast asleep, Katie walked across the room and looked out the window. The rain had let up and everything looked peaceful and still—and safe. "Well, it looks like my two robbery suspects are both innocent," she whispered. "Now all I have to do is face Phoebe and ask her where she got that ten dollar bill." She felt a little shiver up her spine. "I think I'd rather face a purple giant in red shoes!"

At the youth meeting Wednesday night, Katie watched the clock closely. Fifteen minutes before the closing song, she snatched her jacket and started toward the door.

"Do you want me to go with you, Katie?" whispered Tim.

Katie shook her head. This was her problem, and she would take care of it.

As if things weren't bad enough, the fog was back. Katie's knees were knocking against each other when she got outdoors and walked from the brightly lighted church building over to the big house next door. It too was lit, though dimly, and parked cars lined the driveway.

Katie drew a deep breath when she spied the diamond-shaped logo of Mapleton Realty on the door of one car. So that was why the trustees were meeting in Good Sam House tonight. Had Phoebe already convinced them to sell the big house?

Katie's knees stopped knocking. She stepped up on the verandah and pressed the doorbell. She had to do this.

Stormy Fall

A short, bald-headed man, one of the trustees, came to the door. "Yes?" he said impatiently.

"Uh, I'm Katie Barnes, and I need to talk to Mrs. Phillips, please."

"The trustees' committee is meeting at the moment, and Mrs. Phillips is our chairperson. Is this business of yours urgent, young lady?"

"Oh, yes, sir, it is. I need to see her right away."

"All right. Sit down over here and wait."

Katie sat on a small settee in the hall for what seemed a very long time. She could hear Phoebe's harsh voice in the meeting room. Finally, Phoebe burst into the hallway and clumped over to Katie, her cane tapping with each step.

"What do you want, Katie Barnes? What do you mean interrupting our meeting? Don't you realize I'm the chairperson? They can hardly function without me!"

"I'm sorry," Katie said, "but I had something important to ask you and I figured I should do it right away."

"And what is so important?" sneered Phoebe.

"This." Katie reached into her jacket and took out the special ten dollar bill. She held it over to Phoebe. "It's part of the money you gave me two Sundays ago."

"Well, you're not getting one red cent more from me, young lady. You can just march right out that door again!"

"I didn't want more money. I want you to tell me where you got this bill. It's special. See?" Katie turned the bill over to show Alexander Hamilton's engraved picture. She pointed to the printed name, *Sean Patrick*, on either side of the image.

Phoebe snatched the bill from Katie's hand and looked at it closely. "So some vandal defaced a piece of money and

Stormy Fall

you claim it came from me. How could I possibly remember where I obtained a certain ten dollar bill? Are you trying to make a point?"

Katie was tired of being polite. "That bill was one of the three bills you handed me. Now Tim Reilly tells me this bill had belonged to his uncle, Sean Patrick. He put it in the offering plate at the Harvest Dinner. I wondered how you happened to have it, since all that offering money was stolen from the church the next night."

Phoebe gasped. Her long face turned chalk white. She didn't speak for so long, Katie thought she had lost her voice. Then Katie pulled back as Phoebe raised her cane high like a sword and held it there. "You—you are questioning my integrity? You dare to accuse me of taking part in that sordid crime? Go! Go this very minute!" She wildly waved the cane at Katie.

Katie didn't wait around. She dashed for the door, tugged it open, and ran outside.

"Oh, and Katie!" Phoebe hobbled over to the open doorway. "You can tell the other members of your youth group that Mapleton Realty has just offered us a great price for this old house. As soon as the board members begin to see things my way, we'll be ordering the stained-glass windows!"

"They haven't approved it yet!" Katie shouted back as she ran. She put her hands over her ears so she wouldn't have to hear Phoebe's reply. When she got back to the church, she waited outside by the door to catch her breath.

Soon the door opened and kids began trickling out.

Alisha hurried over to her. "I can tell by your face that you talked to Phoebe, Katie. What happened?"

Katie scowled. "She wouldn't say anything about how she

got that bill. All she did was scream at me for questioning her integrity."

"Did she look at the bill?" asked Tim.

"She looked at it, all right. Then I thought she was going to stab me with her cane! She kept the ten dollars, too. We don't even have it for evidence."

"It probably wouldn't have mattered anyway," said Tim sadly. "After all this trouble with two old homeless women, the church board isn't about to put a homeless shelter right next door. We've got to think of something—quick!"

Katie bent her head as she buttoned her coat against the chill. She didn't want the kids to see how bad she was feeling about this news. "I'm just about fresh out of ideas, guys. Phoebe must be the happiest woman in the world tonight."

"I don't know about that," Shad said. "She doesn't look too happy to me."

Everyone looked toward the big house. Phoebe, bundled up in her mink coat, was hobbling as fast as her cane would take her out to her parked car. She tossed the cane onto the empty seat, climbed in, and slammed the door. With a powerful roar, the car backed out to the road and was gone.

In minutes the lights in the big house went out. A small group of men and women slowly walked to their cars.

"What happened?" one of the men called loudly.

"Dunno," said another. "Phoebe said something important had come up and she needed to check it out."

"So what about me?" said a woman's voice. "Should I put a 'For Sale' sign on this house?"

"Better ask Phoebe. She always handles . . ." The voices faded as the group moved farther away.

Stormy Fall

The last of the youth group members came out the door and the light went off inside. There was no shouting and laughing as they walked out toward the parking lot. Shad silently walked past the basketball hoop. Alisha gazed absently into the fog, and Katie studied the ground intently. Even the kids who had opposed the homeless shelter were oddly quiet.

Michael Vincent zipped up his leather jacket as he walked over to join Shad and Tim. "It's kind of weird," he said. "I should be feeling great that there won't be a Good Sam House, but I don't." He looked across the yard toward the empty house. "You know, the other night my dad and I drove by the old underpass and we saw people curled up on the bare ground trying to keep warm." Michael rubbed his hands together to warm them. "I guess it kind of made me think again about this homeless shelter thing."

"I think I know what you mean, Mike," agreed Claudia. "Sometimes on cold nights like this I can't help thinking there really should be a place where homeless people can go to stay warm." She sighed. "I guess I just didn't want it to be next door to our church."

Katie shivered, unsure if it was because of the cold or Claudia's words.

By now, cars were pulling into the church parking lot to pick up the youth group members.

"A homeless shelter would have been a wonderful thing for our church to do," said Sue as the group started moving out toward their cars.

"Stop!" shouted Katie. She felt her face getting hot as everyone turned and stared at her. "You're talking like it's all over. Well, it's not! Good Sam House hasn't been sold yet. Edith and Stella haven't been convicted of a crime, either. Hey, our group's starting to agree that we need Good Sam House! Are we going to give up on God now?"

"No!" shouted the other kids.

Sue began laughing. "Katie, I've always said you'd be a great cheerleader."

"Well, to show how much I agree with you, Katie," said Tim, "on Saturday morning you and I are going down to Ellison Simms's flower shop and buy his prettiest potted plant to hand-deliver to Stella Tootle."

"And the junior high youth group will foot the bill," said Ed Kipper. "But right now, you kids had better head to your cars. There's some parents out there wondering what happened to us."

As usual on the trip home, Katie and Alisha managed to get the rear seat of the Emery's van. "I wonder where Phoebe was going after her meeting?" said Alisha. "She didn't drive toward her home. I watched her leave. She was either heading downtown or to the freeway."

"Well, whatever she's up to, we'll learn about it soon enough," Katie said.

Chapter Sixteen

Phoebe didn't answer her phone the rest of that week.

"Mom said she missed the Thursday afternoon Bible study and the church finance meeting Friday night," said Katie to Tim. It was Saturday morning, and the two of them were walking across town to Ellison Simms's flower shop. "I hope she didn't have another car accident on Wednesday night. I'd feel like it was partly my fault for upsetting her."

"Believe me, Katie, if Phoebe had an accident, the whole church would have heard about it," said Tim. "She's fine."

"You're probably right." Katie shivered and huddled down in her heavy hooded jacket. The harsh wind blew a scattering of leaves and trash across the sidewalk. There was no fog this morning, but dark gray clouds hung low over downtown Mapleton. "Another beautiful Western Washington day, huh?"

Tim grinned. His freckled nose was red from the cold. "Just look at those dark stratus clouds. I predict it's going to start raining again soon. You see, we need . . ."

"Please, Tim," groaned Katie. "Don't give me a lecture on rain this morning."

"Nope, no lectures. But we do need the rain, Katie. All the

lakes and rivers are lower than normal this fall." He looked up at the sky and laughed as the first raindrops of the morning hit his face. "Yep, here it comes! Hurry! We've got to beat this storm!"

Katie tried to take longer strides, but the fierce wind kept pushing her back, and more rain smacked their faces. She felt like she'd been running a marathon by the time they reached the flower shop.

Wind made the green and white striped awnings flap wildly above the windows. A large sign that read "SIMMS'S FINE FLOWERS" banged against the wall. Katie snatched the fancy brass door handle and pulled the door open.

"Get inside!" yelled Tim. He pushed Katie through the doorway and followed her. As the glass door began closing, the huge, heavy sign above pulled loose, crashing down and shattering the plate glass.

"Wow! We can thank God that we made it inside," said Katie in a shaky voice.

"You can say that again," agreed Tim. He turned toward the front counter. "Mr. Simms, I'm afraid . . ." But no one was in sight.

"He must be in back." Katie turned and gazed around the big room crowded with refrigerated display cases. "Look at all these flowers! I don't think I've ever seen so many roses in all my life! And glads, too!" She caught her breath. "See that big pot of yellow chrysanthemums, Tim? They remind me of daffodils. Do you remember Edith and Stella planting all those daffodil bulbs at the church? Let's buy those chrysanthemums for Stella."

"Great idea," said Tim. "But first we'd better find Mr.

Stormy Fall

Simms. He's not going to be happy about what happened to his plate glass window." He rang a small bell on the counter, but no one came out.

"That's weird," said Katie. "The door was unlocked, so someone's here. Maybe he's in the back room. Let's check."

Cautiously, they pushed open a swinging door and peered in. This looked like a workroom with its long counters and stacks of baskets and vases. But no one was in here, either.

"How about this door?" Katie turned to a doorway that was ajar and peeked into an empty office. She walked inside. "Ellison Simms is pretty careless, leaving this shop unlocked with no one to look after it. I'll just write a note and leave it on his desk."

"No, Katie!" Tim said. "We shouldn't even be in here. A sign on the door said 'Private.'"

Katie shrugged. "Okay, then let's just walk to a grocery store and buy Stella a plant. If your mom is going to drive us to the hospital, she'll be getting anxious about us."

Before Tim could answer, they heard a noise out in the sales room. Suddenly, the office door behind them swung shut.

"Someone must have come into the shop," said Tim. "I guess the wind blew this door shut." He sped across the small room and worked the doorknob. "Uh-oh, I think we're locked in!" He pounded on the wooden door. "Mr. Simms? We're locked in your office!" There was no answer.

"Oh, don't get uptight, Tim," said Katie. "Look! There's a phone on the desk. We'll just call the shop number, and when someone answers, we'll explain what happened." She picked up a black cordless phone. "Do you know the phone number?"

"Of course not," said Tim. "We need a phone book."

Katie shuffled papers on top of the desk, then began opening the drawers.

"You shouldn't be snooping in there, Katie!"

"I'm looking for a phone book." Katie slammed one drawer shut and opened another. "We could be here all weekend if no one unlocks this door for us." She opened the bottom drawer and quickly thumbed through a stack of papers. Inside the drawer was a packet of checks, held together with a rubber band. Glancing down at the top check, Katie saw it had been made out to Mapleton Community Church.

Now Katie couldn't help herself. She picked up the packet and looked at each check. "Tim, do you know what this is?"

Tim looked over her shoulder. "I know it's something you shouldn't be looking at, Katie."

Angrily, Katie waved the packet of checks under his freckled nose. "These are the rest of the missing checks from the Harvest Dinner! If Mr. Ellison Simms would show his face right now, we could ask him how he happens to have them."

Tim snatched the phone receiver. "Quiet, Katie! I'm calling Mom to come down and help us get out of this mess. We could be in real danger!"

"I'll take that phone!" said a voice behind them.

Katie jumped up so fast, she cracked her head on a corner of the desk. She stared straight into the long face of Ellison Simms. In his right hand he held a small gun. Surely it was only a toy, but it looked very real. In his left hand he clutched a ring of keys. "I don't know what this town's coming to," he said. "I slip next door briefly to buy a latte, and what do I find upon my return? A pair of thieves! You two shatter my glass door, then sneak into my private office!"

Stormy Fall

"The wind blew your sign down and smashed the door," protested Katie. "We came to buy a plant, and we got locked in here, then . . ." She couldn't say any more.

Tim stepped up bravely. "We rang the bell on the counter, but no one answered."

The angry florist sneered, stuffing the key ring into his vest pocket. "I wonder what the police will say about those weak excuses for breaking and entering." He aimed the gun toward Katie. "But first, young lady, you'd better give those to me." Laying the phone down, he snatched the packet of checks from Katie's hand.

"I'll just tell the police you have those checks when they get here," threatened Katie.

Ellison laughed. "Do you really think the police will believe a pair of teenage thieves from Lower Mapleton?" He crammed the checks in his coat pocket and picked up the phone again.

"You won't need to make that call, Mr. Simms," rumbled a deep voice. "We're right behind you."

The phone crashed to the floor. All three of them turned at once and stared at the doorway. Katie had never known that blue uniforms and shiny badges could look so good.

"Mr. Sergeyev! Man, am I glad to see you!" shouted Tim. He beamed over at Katie. "Officer Sergeyev lives across the street from us." Tim glanced over at Ellison Simms. "In Lower Mapleton."

Officer Sergeyev's ruddy face crinkled into a smile. "I'm glad to see you, too, Tim. My wife just called me on her cell phone. Your mom was getting concerned that you two were taking so long to buy your plant. She couldn't check on you herself, so she wondered if we might be in the area. It just so happens, we were."

"And I'd say it's a good thing, too," said his partner, a stocky blond man who looked like he wouldn't take any nonsense from anyone. He scowled as he eyed the small gun in Ellison's hand.

Mr. Simms drew himself up to his full six-foot height. "I can explain this gun, sir. But first, I want to press charges against these two young hoodlums! While I was next door for a few minutes, purchasing a latte, they smashed my expensive plate-glass door, sneaked into the shop, and were rummaging through my desk!" He slipped the gun into his pocket. "I do have a permit for the gun, of course."

"He just put some stolen checks from our church dinner in his vest pocket!" accused Katie.

The blond officer held out his hand. "Sir, if we can just have that packet of checks . . ."

Ellison's long face turned the color of skim milk. "I . . . I'm not giving you anything if you don't have a search warrant." He looked toward the phone. "I think I'd better call my attorney."

"Fine," said Officer Sergeyev. "You can tell him to meet you down at the police station. But for now, you have the right to remain silent. Anything you say can and will be used against you in a court of law. You have the right to an attorney. If you cannot afford one, one will be appointed for you."

"But this is just some terrible misunderstanding," protested Ellison. "Why, I've even changed my mind. I'm not going to press charges against this pair."

Katie placed her hands on her hips as she stared up into

Stormy Fall

his face. "So what about your cousin Phoebe? Is she in on this crime, too?"

"There is no crime!" said the angry florist. "And my dear cousin would vouch for me on every account, I assure you! Oh, of all the times for her to go to Boston!" He was still fuming as he was ushered out the door and into the back seat of the waiting patrol car.

The police offered Katie and Tim a ride home, but the two chose to walk in spite of the weather.

"If we need to talk to you later, we'll get in touch," said Officer Sergeyev.

After the patrol car had pulled away, Katie turned to Tim. "I don't believe a word that man says, Tim. I don't think Phoebe suddenly went to Boston. Something's wrong and we should go check on her."

"Katie, aren't we in enough trouble?" asked Tim. "Mr. Simms could still press charges against us."

"That man's not going to press charges against anyone," said Katie. "He's going to be too busy explaining how he happened to have that packet of checks! Let's go see if Phoebe's home. No one's seen her or talked to her since Wednesday night."

Tim scratched his head. "That sounds crazy, but, hey, Mom's gonna drive us over to the hospital anyway. Maybe she won't mind a short detour. Come on!"

By now, rain was streaming down and the wind howled like someone in pain. When they finally arrived, soaking wet, at Tim's house, Mrs. Reilly was pacing the floor. "I was about ready to start looking for you two kids. This storm is terrible." She pulled on her heavy jacket. "Well, let's go. My neighbor is looking after the little ones."

"Mrs. Reilly, could we take a detour up to Phoebe's house first?" Katie asked.

"Well, I suppose so," Mrs. Reilly said.

"Katie thinks she might be in trouble," Tim said.

Mrs. Reilly's eyebrows rose. "Well sure, we can stop by and see her. Are you guys going to fill me in on the way?"

"Definitely," said Katie. The three of them piled in the car and started off toward Phoebe's house. The windshield wipers swished at full speed against the rain.

"I've been to Phoebe's lots of times to help with her spring cleaning," Mrs. Reilly told them. "Of course, I always had to use the back door." She chuckled.

Within a few minutes, Mrs. Reilly drove down the long, tree-lined driveway and pulled to a stop. The branches swayed as if beckoning them toward the big house. Tim and Katie jumped from the car and dashed up the front steps to the pillared verandah.

Katie rang the chiming doorbell again and again, but there was no sound inside.

"Come on, Katie, let's go. She's not home," Tim said.

"No, wait!" Katie laid her ear against the door. "I think I hear a thumping sound. Maybe Phoebe has fallen down and can't get up again!" She turned to Tim. "Go get a rock or something. We'll break a window."

"No way, Katie! I'm not gonna spend the night in jail!" Tim said.

"Hold it, kids," called Mrs. Reilly from the foot of the steps. "Mrs. Phillips used to keep a spare key on the ledge above her kitchen door. I'll go check."

But Katie raced back down the cement steps and beat her

Stormy Fall

to the back door. She fumbled anxiously on the high ledge above the door, finally grasping the spare key. Fitting it into the lock, she gave the key a twist and shoved the door open, then ran through the kitchen and down the long, carpeted hallway.

The thumping sound was louder here. Katie finally reached Phoebe's room and eased the door open. She stared.

A weak, dirty, foul-smelling Phoebe Phillips half sat, half lay on the floor beside her big bed. She waved a hand at Katie.

"Ellison—Ellison drugged me!" she gasped, and toppled over onto the floor.

Mrs. Reilly and Tim came running down the hallway. "Let's get her up off the floor!" shouted Mrs. Reilly. "Katie, call her doctor!"

By the time Dr. Bliss had arrived, Phoebe had been bathed and changed into a clean nightgown. Now she lay propped up in bed in her guest room. When she heard her doctor's voice, she struggled to sit up. "Katie, hand me my comb and mirror. I must look a sight!"

The story she told them, as she sipped chicken noodle soup, was a sad one. After talking with Katie Wednesday night, Phoebe had driven straight to Ellison's condominium to demand that he tell her the truth.

"It was that ten dollar bill," she said in a husky voice. "I knew I had gotten those bills in change from Ellison just before I saw you. I had stopped in to buy a bouquet of flowers for Berniece's birthday." Tears rolled down her long, pale face. "He . . . he laughed at me. He actually said he thought I'd be glad those two old women would get the blame and the church would be rid of them."

Stormy Fall

"But why did Ellison take that money?" asked Mrs. Reilly as she held a box of tissues out to Phoebe. "Surely he didn't need it."

"No, he simply wanted to ensure that Good Samaritan House never happened." Her hand trembled as she tugged a tissue from the box. "He said he was making sure that our church was not overrun by common criminals and decrepit homeless people. In his own twisted way, he was just trying to do what he thought was best for the church." She blew her nose. "I told Ellison he must tell the police what he had done. Then I left and drove home."

"So how did you get in this mess?" asked Katie.

Phoebe leaned her head back against the pillow and closed her eyes. "He came to my house late that night. He took my cane, ripped out the phone lines, and forced me to drink a cup of hot tea. He wasn't like my Ellison at all. He was . . . he was like a *madman!*"

Tears trickled down from her closed eyes.

"The last three days, I've lain here helplessly. Each night Ellison would come back and force me to eat a meal and drink a cup of tea. I knew the tea was drugged, but I was too weak to stop him." She moaned and turned her face to the wall. "Last night," she said in a voice that was almost a whisper, "I saw a gun in Ellison's overcoat pocket. I . . . I'm afraid he was trying to get up the nerve to shoot me. *Me,* his own cousin!" Phoebe began crying, big sobs that shook her body. "I would have done anything for Ellison."

The doctor motioned for all of them to leave the room. "Let's let her sleep now," said the doctor. "She's had a terrible experience."

Stormy Fall

Tim and Katie didn't get to visit Stella in the hospital until Sunday afternoon. They took her a nice chrysanthemum plant that they'd bought at a nearby Safeway.

A pale Stella lay there in her bed, motionless, during their visit. Katie sat on a chair beside the bed and took Stella's rough, gnarled hand in hers. "Everything's all right now, Stella," she said. "Everyone knows you and Edith didn't do anything wrong." She squeezed the old woman's hand, but Stella didn't squeeze back. Her eyelids remained tightly closed.

Chapter Seventeen

"*M*om! Dad!" Katie came clattering down downstairs on Thanksgiving morning, Hannah at her heels. "Look out the window at the blue sky! The stormy weather has ended."

Dad chuckled. "It sure has, girls. I believe we're going to have a perfect Thanksgiving day."

"And a busy one," added Mom, stepping from the kitchen as she wiped her hands on a towel. "You both had better go upstairs and get dressed. We'll need your help."

At two that afternoon, the sky was still blue and Katie was so busy, she'd hardly had a minute to sit down. Now, she watched as her mom and dad each took a handle of the heavy roasting pan and lugged a giant golden-brown turkey from the oven over to the kitchen table. When someone pounded at the kitchen door, she hurried to answer it.

"Happy Thanksgiving!" shouted Mark Gomez as he, his folks, and his little sister, Marita, stepped into the warm kitchen. Mark's eyes gleamed as he saw the loaded table. "Man, that's gotta be about the biggest turkey I've ever seen."

Katie laughed. "Doesn't it look great? Dad's boss surprised all his employees with a free turkey for Thanksgiving."

"And the first thing we did was invite all our good friends and neighbors over for Thanksgiving dinner," added Mom,

Stormy Fall

as she took a big covered platter from Mrs. Gomez. "Mmm, this smells good. I hope it's a platter of those famous Gomez tamales."

"Specially made." Mrs. Gomez's broad smile nearly split her face in two. "We closed the Los Amigos Café for Thanksgiving after we got your kind invitation, Sarah."

But now a second car had pulled into the driveway, and another family came hurrying across the yard. "Don't close the door on us, Katie!" called Alisha Asher.

"I'd never close the door on you, Alisha." Katie gave her friend a giant hug. "I thought you had to go to your Aunt Salome's for Thanksgiving."

Alisha made a face. "That's what we were going to do, but Aunt Salome and one of her friends decided to drive down to California and see if they can find cushy jobs for the winter." Alisha's face lit up in a conspiratorial grin. "I'm glad it worked out this way," she whispered in Katie's ear. "Aunt Salome's a lousy cook."

"I'm glad, too," said Katie. "Without the Tootle sisters being here today, we were afraid we wouldn't have any company."

While Dad helped everyone take off their coats and go into the living room, Mom stayed behind to answer the ringing phone.

". . . Yes? . . . Oh, Sean's not feeling well? I'm sorry to hear that. . . . Well, of course we still want you to come today." Mom hung up the phone and turned to Katie. "It seems the Reilly family will be here for dinner after all. Tim's Uncle Sean is in bed with a terrible sinus headache because of all the rain, so they can't go to his house today."

"Good! Hannah will love having the little Reilly girls." Katie

Stormy Fall

turned away to hide her own happy smile. Not because she was glad Tim's family couldn't be with their relatives this year, but because . . . well, just because.

"Oh, and Idah Emery called last night to tell me they'll be in Seattle today, but they hope to share leftovers with us tomorrow." Mom laughed. "I guess their nephew, Charley, wants me to be sure and save him some sweet potato casserole. It's just a miracle how that boy's changing, isn't it?"

Katie nodded. "It sure is." She looked out the window as another car turned into their driveway.

"Here comes Skip!" yelled Alex from the living room. The front door banged as he ran outside to greet his friend.

It was nearly three in the afternoon when everyone was seated around two big makeshift tables in the living room. Katie was slightly embarrassed that the tables were covered with Mom's big white sheets. Still, these folks were all good friends. They wouldn't care that the Barneses couldn't afford real tablecloths.

When the phone rang again, Katie jumped up. "You stay here, Mom. I'll answer it this time." She hurried to the kitchen. It was nearly ten minutes before she joined her family and friends again.

Mom walked over to her. "Who was on the phone, Katie? Is something wrong?"

"It was Gwen Van Switt. Would you believe it, Mom? She asked if she and her mother could come here for dinner today."

"What? Aren't they having dinner with Gwen's aunt and uncle?"

Katie shrugged helplessly. "I guess not. Gwen said her rela-

Stormy Fall

tives went to Oregon and left her and her mom here alone. It sounds like Gwen's mother was starting to drink again because she's depressed."

"Oh, dear," said Mom. "I've got to call and tell Mrs. Van Switt that they're welcome to join us today."

Katie sighed, clear down to her toes. "You needn't bother, Mom. I knew you'd say that, so I already invited them. They'll be here in about fifteen minutes."

"Fifteen minutes?" yipped Mark. "I don't know if I can wait that long!"

"Why, Mark Gomez," scolded his mother. "We're all going to sit here and patiently wait. That poor woman needs our support today."

"Thanks, folks, for being so understanding," said Mom. She laid a hand on Katie's shoulder. "And thank you, Katie. Sometimes the right thing to do isn't the easiest."

"Yeah," mumbled Katie.

When Mrs. Van Switt's small red sports car wheeled into the driveway a little later, Katie and her mom walked out to meet them. Katie watched Mrs. Van Switt climb out and come toward them, weaving as she walked. Then Gwen took her mother's arm and gently helped her up onto the front porch.

Katie couldn't help feeling pity for the girl. *Poor Gwen. It must be hard taking care of your mother instead of your mother looking after you.* "Please, God," she quietly prayed. "Help me to be more patient with Gwen. She can be such a pain. And thanks for protecting Gwen and her mom during their drive here, Lord. Keep them safe."

"Hi, Katie," Gwen said, smiling at her.

"Hi, Gwen. Welcome to our house." Katie took the blond

Stormy Fall

girl's stylish coat. Her dad helped Mrs. Van Switt to an empty chair, and Mom handed her a cup of strong black coffee.

Gwen sat down beside Katie and batted her blue eyes at Tim Reilly across the table. "So nice to see you, Tim," she cooed. Gwen glanced down at the table. "My goodness, Katie, do you always use bed sheets for tablecloths at your house?"

Katie felt the old anger boiling up inside her. Then she remembered what she had prayed a few minutes earlier. She smiled sweetly. "Only on Thanksgiving day, Gwen."

Now that their last two guests were seated, Dad looked all around at everyone and beamed happily. "Well, I believe we're all here now." His wide smile faded. "Except for two sweet little ladies who couldn't be here."

Katie thought of Edith and Stella Tootle and felt a big lump rise in her throat.

"Anyway," Dad's big voice went on, "let's join hands and thank the good Lord for all the blessings we do have." When his prayer ended, a chorus of "Amens" sounded throughout the crowded living room.

The tender roast turkey was soon carved and passed around, and Mark was reaching for a bowl of cranberry sauce when a sharp knock sounded at the door.

"Now who can that be?" Dad asked.

This time, Alex was first to the door. He swung it wide. After a quick glance at the new arrival, he turned back with his mouth open and his eyes wide. "It's Phoebe Phillips!"

"What?" Dad pushed his chair back and joined Alex.

"Why—why, Mrs. Phillips! Come on in!" he said. "We're just getting started with our feast."

The room fell silent as Phoebe Phillips, wearing her flowing mink coat and aided by her cane, clumped inside. Then, looking back out the doorway, she said, "Well, hurry up!" She turned to Dad. "This person insists she was invited here for Thanksgiving."

Every pair of eyes stared and every mouth hung open as a tiny gray-haired woman, wearing "missionary barrel" clothes, bounced into the house. A dirty, faded Mariners baseball cap was perched on her head.

"Edith!" gasped a roomful of astonished people. "It's Edith Tootle!"

Katie and Alisha pushed back their chairs and zigzagged around the tables. They both wrapped up the little woman in a mighty sandwich hug.

"Oh, Edith, where've you been?" Katie asked. "We thought you were dead!"

"Dead!" Edith chortled. "I don't think so, Katie." She shook her head. "Though I gotta admit, I sure didn't know who I was or where I was 'til last night when those nice policemen rescued me and my new friends."

"Rescued them!" Phoebe butted in. "The police *arrested* Edith and her so-called friends for loitering in the back alleys of Tacoma."

"Tacoma? Edith, how'd you end up in Tacoma?" asked Mrs. Reilly.

"It seems a certain snake in the grass drove me over there and dumped me after he figured out that I'd lost my memory." Edith looked apologetically at Phoebe Phillips. "Now, I'm sorry, dear. I know that rascal's your cousin, but from what I hear, he didn't have nothin' good in mind for you either."

Edith looked around at the roomful of people and her

eyes got big. "I remember everything about that awful night now. Stella and me heard a noise in the church. We sneaked up from the basement and saw that fellow, Ellison Simms, taking all the moneybags from the church safe. We knew he shouldn't have done that. When he started for the outside door, we took after him. I guess that's when we tripped over each other and tumbled down the stairs."

She took a not-very-clean hankie from her ancient tweed coat pocket and blew her nose. "Poor Stella. I lost my memory, but she got hurt worse." Edith's face brightened. "But she was looking and sounding pretty good when we visited her today, wasn't she, Phoebe?"

"You've seen Stella?" asked Mom. "How is she? Is she conscious yet?" While she was still asking questions, she seated Edith in an empty chair.

"I should say so," said Phoebe, with a ladylike snort. "She's been doing fine ever since she saw this one. Keeps saying, 'I told you not to chase that crook, Edith.'" Phoebe made a clicking sound with her tongue. "Finally, the nurse had us leave before Edith talked the poor soul to death."

"Mighty sorry she couldn't come for dinner, though," added Edith.

"Well, now, before we do any more talking, we want you both to sit down and eat," said Mom. "I'll fix a plate to send to Stella." Mom tried to help Phoebe out of her fur coat, but Phoebe pulled away.

"*I'm* not staying here for dinner," she said. "I'm only here because Pastor Miller called me this morning to tell me Edith was in custody at the Mapleton jail. He knew how worried I was that Ellison would be arrested for her murder. Ellison

Stormy Fall

has signed a complete confession, you know. We'll be spared the embarrassment of a trial."

"Little enough to do," muttered Edith.

Phoebe glared at the interruption. "Anyway, after Edith's release, I told Pastor Miller we wouldn't waste money on a motel room again and offered to let her use my basement apartment. We stopped at the hospital first to visit Stella."

Edith took off her grubby cap and waved it. "The police gave me back my cap, too. That rascal, Ellison, figured he'd make me look guilty by tossing it and some stolen checks into the Green River. I guess it looks pretty dirty now." She plopped the cap back on her wiry gray hair.

No one sitting around the two Thanksgiving tables had eaten another bite of food. They all sat on the edge of their chairs, thrilled by this unbelievable story. Katie did notice Mr. Young slip quietly out the front door and then back in while Edith and Phoebe talked.

Now, holding a small bag, he walked up to Edith and took out a brand new Mariners baseball cap. "This is for you, Edith." He handed the cap to her. "I bought it at the last baseball game I went to."

"Why—why thank you, sir." Tears rolled down Edith's wrinkled cheeks. She tugged off her old cap and began to unfasten the small, tarnished cross. The back of the pin snapped off and the broken cross tumbled to the floor. Edith looked down sadly. "Well, shoot. I guess that's the end of my pin. I might as well throw it away now."

"Don't worry. We'll buy you a new one," promised Tim.

Katie scooped up the tarnished cross. "If you don't want this, Edith, I'll keep it. I know just where I'll put it."

Stormy Fall

"Honey, it's yours," said Edith.

Phoebe had been looking around the room and seemed surprised when she spied Gwen's mother sitting beside Mrs. Reilly. "Why, Caroline Van Switt, what are you doing here? I understood you were too 'under the weather' to go to Oregon with your family for Thanksgiving."

Mrs. Van Switt's face turned red, but she managed a smile as she took another sip of black coffee. "Oh, I'm feeling much better today, Phoebe, and we're having a wonderful time."

Phoebe sniffed and pulled her mink coat closer about her. "Well, I'll be going then."

"Now, Phoebe, we'd be honored if you stayed and ate with us," coaxed Dad.

Phoebe stopped in her tracks. "How can you say that, Harvey Barnes? How could you be honored to have me stay for dinner when you know my cousin is . . . is a jail bird?" She looked around the room again. "What are you trying to do today—have a gathering of all the misfits of Mapleton?" Her long face twisted as if she were going to cry.

"Certainly not," said Mom. She came over and again began to take off Phoebe's mink coat. "This is a Thanksgiving dinner for us and our friends, and we're all here to give thanks and praise the Lord. Now, sit down, Phoebe," and Mom gave her a gentle shove into another empty chair.

It was nearly dark when the ladies cut and served the pumpkin, apple, and mincemeat pies. Katie followed behind, putting a glop of whipped cream on each piece.

"Goodness," said Phoebe, the reluctant guest, as she finished her second piece of pie. "I feel positively stuffed." She glanced out the window. "Edith, we must be leaving for my house soon. It's dark outside."

"Begging your pardon, Phoebe," said the spunky little lady, "but I won't be going to your house. Since Stella and me'll be living at Good Sam House, I figured I'd just bunk there tonight. That way I can get an early start on my cleaning job at the church tomorrow morning."

Katie stood still. "Oh, Edith, didn't anyone tell you? There isn't going to be a Good Samaritan House."

"Of course there is," said Edith.

"Of course there is," echoed Phoebe.

Katie's head swerved from one woman to the other. "Huh? But, Phoebe—the trustees? The church board?"

Phoebe shrugged as if these details were of no importance. "I called the other trustees this morning and, naturally, they all agree with me that we need the homeless shelter. And don't worry about the church board. I can turn them around, too."

Katie sat the bowl of whipped topping on the table. "But, Phoebe, you didn't want a homeless shelter next to the church building."

"Katie, dear," said Phoebe, as though she was talking to a stubborn child, "I had a lot of time to think during those long days and nights while I was held prisoner in my home. Then, when you and your friends came and rescued me—maybe saved my life—I knew for sure. How could there be any better place for needy people than to be right beside a church full of Christian people who want to help them." She smiled up at the shocked Katie. "Now, be a dear, and give me another dollop of whipped cream on my pie, please?"

Stormy Fall

It was nine-thirty that night when the Reillys, the last of the dinner guests, piled into their old car.

"Hey, Katie," called Tim, "I hope you're not going to tell me all these good things are happening just because the fog ended and the rain started up."

Katie laughed. "No, Tim, I'll admit you were right about the fog. It kind of made me feel down in the dumps, but it wasn't at fault for the bad things that were happening in Mapleton."

She walked out to the Reillys's car—it was raining again—and leaned her folded arms on the open car window. "I think there's another kind of 'fog,' though, that keeps people from being friends—prejudice. It makes well-to-do people look at the poor folks, and all they can see are unwashed, ignorant thieves."

Tim grinned back at her. "Yeah, and sometimes poor folks look at rich folks up on the hill and all they can see are snobs who only care about themselves."

"Oh, that hits home all right, Tim. So let's hope we're rid of the fog around here for a while."

"Yeah," agreed Tim. "Now, you'd better run into your house, Katie, before you wash away. See ya."

"Yeah. See ya." Katie ran up to the porch and watched Mrs. Reilly start up the car and slowly pull out of the driveway. Then Katie squeezed the raindrops out of her short dark hair, turned, and went inside.

The Barnes family unanimously agreed to wait until the next morning to make their Thanksgiving telephone call to Sunnydale. "I'm afraid they'd be shocked to get a call in the middle of the night," said Mom.

"If we can get that free Internet service for our computer, we can send messages anytime," said Alex.

When Katie crept up to her room, Hannah was sound asleep in her bed. Katie undressed quietly. Suddenly, she remembered something. Reaching in the pocket of her yellow sweater, she took out the tiny broken cross. Tip-toeing across the creaky floor, she laid the cross on the dresser while she picked up the small, hand-carved chest sitting there. She tipped the chest on its side and pushed the lever on the bottom. A secret drawer slowly creaked open. Inside, Katie saw a small rock, a snapshot of Little Mike as a baby pup, a pressed yellow rose, and a blue-jay feather. She picked up the broken cross and laid it in the open drawer with her other family treasures.

"Someday, Grandma Ross and I will sit down together and look at each one of these things and talk about them," Katie whispered to herself. Carefully, she closed the secret drawer and put the chest back on top of her dresser. Then, pulling on her baggy pajamas, she said her prayers and went to sleep.

All Katie Barnes ever wanted to be was a normal teen ...

"Oh, of course we're not gypsies," Katie said. "We're a perfectly normal family from Sunnydale, Kansas, and we just moved out here to Washington." Katie snatched Hannah's hand and began tugging her toward the sandy path. "And I must say," she blurted, "I'm beginning to wonder why my parents ever decided to come to Washington in the first place."

Book #1

Gypsy Summer

Betty Barclift

Between Two Worlds
LeAnne Hardy

When Cristina moves to Minnesota from Brazil, she feels like she doesn't fit in. The kids in school make fun of her and she doesn't know the latest fashion styles or slang. Missing her friends in Brazil, she wonders if she'll ever be happy again. Then she becomes friends with Jason, a Korean guy also outside the popular circle, and together they discover God's plan for them between the two worlds that they know.

Parker Twins Series
Jeanette Windle

Don't Miss Any of These High Octane Adventures!

Cave of the Inca Re
Jungle Hideout
Captured in Colombia
Mystery at Death Canyon
Secret of the Dragon Mark
Race for the Secret Code